'Maybe you'r[...]

James shot a laug[...]
yet his eyes were oddly intent when they [...]
to her face once more. 'No sign of a ring, I
see, although a lot of people don't bother with
that nowadays. Most couples I know are quite
happy to live together until the urge to name
the big day hits them.'

Elizabeth took a deep breath, wondering why
she was letting such nonsense disturb her. It
was just the strange way that James was
looking at her...as though her answer really
mattered to him! 'I am not "spoken for". Nor
am I living with anyone. I hardly think that
would be appropriate behaviour for someone
in my position!'

'Meaning that the good people of this town
would be shocked?' James laughed softly and
yet there seemed to be a trace of satisfaction in
his deep voice.

Dear Reader

One of the joys of writing is the opportunity it gives you to create new characters, so you can imagine my delight when I was asked to create a whole town!

Yewdale is purely the product of my imagination but during the course of writing this series the characters who live there became very real to me. Gruff old Isaac Shepherd, nosy Marion Rimmer, the Jackson family with their frequent crises... I would sit down at the typewriter each morning, eager to discover what was happening in their lives.

Writing this series has been quite simply a delight. I have had the pleasure of not only bringing together each couple and watching them fall in love, but of seeing how their lives were enriched by the people around them. I hope that you enjoy reading the books as much as I have enjoyed writing them.

My very best wishes to you.

Jennifer Taylor

MARRYING HER PARTNER

BY
JENNIFER TAYLOR

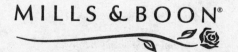

MILLS & BOON®

First published in Great Britain 1999
Harlequin Mills & Boon Limited,
Eton House, 18-24 Paradise Road, Richmond, Surrey TW9 1SR

© Jennifer Taylor 1999

ISBN 0 263 81679 6

Set in Times Roman 10½ on 11½ pt.
03-9905-55252-D

Printed and bound in Norway
by AIT Trondheim AS, Trondheim

CHAPTER ONE

'I HOPE you aren't expecting very much tonight!'

Dr Elizabeth Allen picked up the coffee-pot and filled a mug. She carried it back to her room and set it down on the desk with a thud. 'A glass of wine, cheese, some crackers...'

'That's fine, Liz. Nobody is expecting you to go to a lot of trouble.' David Ross, her partner in the practice, gave her a placatory smile as he came into the room. 'I just thought it would be a nice idea for us all to get together and welcome James to his new job. It will be a big change for him, working here, after London.'

'It will. There's no doubt about that.' Elizabeth sighed as she ran a hand through her auburn hair to push the springy waves back from her face. Her hazel eyes were shadowed as she went to the window. A fine rain was falling that morning, obscuring the view of the nearby hills. The sight was so familiar, though, that she didn't need to see it to picture how the land rose beyond the town in a sweep of soft green.

She'd lived in the small Cumbrian town of Yewdale all her life and loved it with a passion of which few suspected her capable. Cool, calm, composed... Elizabeth knew how people viewed her and it was an image she was happy to foster, preferring to hide her feelings rather than putting them on show. However, it was difficult to hide them now as she turned back to David.

'Do you honestly think Sinclair will fit in? He's never worked in a rural practice like this so he has no experience of the sort of problems he's likely to encounter here. Oh, he's highly qualified, I'll grant you, but doesn't it bother you that he's going to meet situations here which he would never have to cope with in London?'

'No, it doesn't bother me at all. I'm convinced that James Sinclair will not only adapt to the demands of the job but will prove himself invaluable to the practice.' David sighed. 'I hope you're not having second thoughts, Liz. It's a bit late in the day for that. You should have said if you didn't want to offer James the partnership, although, in all honesty, I can't see what you're worried about.'

Second thoughts? Elizabeth sighed as she turned to look out of the window again. In the past two months she'd had second and *third* thoughts about the wisdom of taking on James Sinclair as a partner! She couldn't understand why she had such doubts about him. His qualifications were second to none and the experience he'd gained, working in a busy London practice, had put him streets ahead of the other candidates they'd seen.

David had been jubilant at finding someone of Sinclair's calibre so quickly. They'd been under a lot of pressure since Elizabeth's father had been forced to retire, and she knew that was why she'd gone along with the decision to offer Sinclair the partnership when it was obvious that none of the other applicants could match him. Yet ever since the contracts had been signed she'd worried about it.

Why? Because she wasn't convinced that James Sinclair would adapt to the role of country GP? What basis was there for thinking that, apart from this feeling she had? It was hardly professional to base such a judgement on feminine intuition!

'I'm sure you're right.' She managed a smile as she turned, instantly contrite when she saw the concern on

David's face. He didn't need her worries on top of everything else he had to contend with. 'It's just me, worrying unnecessarily, I expect. James Sinclair will undoubtedly turn out to be the answer to our prayers!'

'Well, I wouldn't go so far as to claim that, but I do hope to make things easier around here.'

There was amusement in the deep voice that brought Elizabeth swinging round. She felt the colour rush to her face as she realised that James Sinclair was standing in the doorway. How much of the conversation had he heard? she wondered. She had no idea, but there was something about the expression in his blue eyes that held a hint of challenge despite the smile he gave her.

'James! Good to see you.' David went to shake hands, making up for Elizabeth's silence with the genuine warmth of his greeting. 'When did you arrive? We weren't sure when to expect you.'

'Late last light.' James Sinclair came into the room and looked around, before letting his gaze come to rest on Elizabeth again. 'I must thank you for arranging that room for me at the pub. I got here later than I expected so I was glad that I didn't have to start looking for a place to stay.'

'David made the arrangements so it's him you should thank, not me.' Elizabeth saw his brows rise and flushed again as she realised he'd caught the faint antagonism in her tone.

She avoided his gaze, taking rapid stock of the immaculate navy suit he was wearing with a pale blue shirt and burgundy silk tie.

The expensive cut of the suit emphasised the lean muscularity of his body, while the soft blue of the shirt set off a tan which he could never have got in England at this time of the year. The colour was also the perfect foil for his fair hair, which was brushed back smoothly from a face which would have been almost too handsome if it hadn't been for that faint crook in his nose.

He looked like what he was, Elizabeth decided finally, suave, sophisticated, citified. Was that why she had these doubts about him—because she couldn't believe that he would be happy, living and working in a small town like Yewdale?

It was only when she realised that he was subjecting her to an equally thorough scrutiny that she turned away, her heart beating a shade faster than it should have been although she couldn't for the life of her understand why.

'Then, thanks again, David. I appreciate the trouble you went to,' James said smoothly, as he turned to the older man with a warm smile.

'Oh, don't mention it.' David brushed aside his thanks. 'Staying there will give you time to look around for a place of your own. In fact, you won't go far wrong if you have a word with Harry Shaw, the publican at the Fleece. He usually has an inside track on which properties are coming on the market. Just one of his many little sidelines, so to speak!'

James laughed softly. 'One of the joys of small towns, I imagine. People know what's going on around them...unlike big cities.' He turned an amused glance on Elizabeth, who was listening silently to what was being said. 'I lived in my last flat for three years and I still have no idea who lived next door to me all that time! I think I'm going to enjoy getting to know everyone in this town and becoming part of the community.'

'Perhaps.' Elizabeth's smile was cool as she sat at her desk. 'But will you enjoy everyone knowing who *you* are? That's an aspect of the job which many find difficult to cope with. You can't just cut off when you live in a town like Yewdale. People stop you in the street, in the shops—in the pub even—to ask your advice or discuss their treatment. Do you think you'll find that easy to deal with? Or a little bit suffocating, as a lot of outsiders do?'

'I imagine time will tell one way or the other.' His tone was bland enough but Elizabeth saw the sparks that lit his blue eyes with an inner fire. 'I'm willing to wait and see, but are you, Elizabeth? Seems to me you've already decided that I might not be up to the job.'

'Nonsense! Liz is just being, well…realistic, I suppose.' David immediately tried to pour oil on troubled waters. He looked at Elizabeth for support, obviously expecting her to add something, but for the life of her she couldn't dredge up a word of reassurance. It was a relief when the buzzer on her desk sounded and she was able to bring the meeting to a close, although she knew that wasn't the end of it.

James Sinclair was going to be living and working in this town from now on, and from necessity they'd be brought into daily contact. She wasn't sure she liked the idea but, equally, couldn't understand why it should disturb her so.

'Sounds like my first patient has arrived,' she said, avoiding his eyes because the realisation troubled her. 'Would you show James which consulting room he'll be using, David, if you don't mind?'

'Of course.' David led the way from the room but James Sinclair lingered so that Elizabeth was forced to look at him.

'I don't know why you have doubts about me, Liz,' he said quietly, putting a delicate emphasis on the shortened form of her name, 'but I hope you'll try to keep an open mind. This job is what I want and I intend to make a success of it, believe me!'

He gave a soft laugh but Elizabeth heard the determination it held. 'I believe a person is innocent until proven guilty under British law. Maybe you should bear that in mind.'

Elizabeth took a small breath as he left the room, unaware until that moment that she'd been holding it. She pressed the buzzer on her desk to inform Eileen Pierce; the receptionist, that she was ready for her first patient, but she was aware that her hand was shaking just a little. She laid it flat on the desk until the tremor passed. She wouldn't allow herself to think about its cause—six feet of designer-clad elegance by the name of Sinclair!

'Right, Mr Shepherd, you can get dressed now. Can you manage or do you need a hand?'

'Don't need no woman helping me!' Isaac Shepherd glared with annoyance at the mere suggestion that he couldn't cope. Elizabeth bit back a sigh as she left him to it. Isaac Shepherd's problem was that he was too proud and stubborn to accept help.

'So, how is he, then, Doc? Silly old beggar should know better than to try doing it all by himself!' Frank, Isaac's son, glared at the screen that hid his father from view. He raised his voice to make sure the old man could hear what he said. 'I told him I'd be up this weekend to help fetch in the ewes, but could he wait till then? Things have to be done right when he wants them done. Since Ma died he's become impossible to reason with!'

'I understand how difficult it must be, Frank.' Elizabeth sat at her desk and glanced at the notes spread before her. It had been over three months since Isaac Shepherd had been into the surgery, far too long in view of his angina. He'd been due to come in on a monthly basis, but repeated phone calls, setting up appointments, had been ignored.

If they hadn't been so busy Elizabeth would have risked paying him a visit on the off chance she might catch him in, but there hadn't been enough time to make the long drive out to the farm, possibly for nothing. Now she gave Frank Shepherd a commiserating smile.

'Your father is a very independent man, Frank.'

'Too damned independent!' Frank snorted. 'I've told him that Jeannie and I are only too happy to have him come live with us, but will he listen…?'

'And what point would there be in me moving in with you? Can't run the farm from town, can I?' Isaac came from behind the screen and glared at his son. 'I was born on that there farm and I'll die on it. That's as should be. The pity is that once I'm gone there'll be nobody to take over from me!'

'Sit down, Mr Shepherd,' Elizabeth cut in hurriedly, knowing how quickly the conversation could deteriorate into another argument. It was a bone of contention between father and son that Frank had moved into town to work at the small pottery that made giftware for the tourists who flooded the area in the summer months. However, her main concern was to make Isaac see that he couldn't go on disregarding his illness, without it having disastrous consequences.

'Look, Mr Shepherd, there isn't an easy way of saying this so I may as well give it to you straight—you can't carry on, running that farm, all by yourself. Physically, it's just too much for you.'

'I've done it all my life! There's nowt that needs to be done I can't handle!' the old man retorted.

'It would be hard enough for a man your age even if he was in perfect health, which you're not. Whether you're willing to accept it or not, your angina must be taken into consideration.' Elizabeth fixed the old man with a level stare.

'I explained all that to you the last time I saw you— how the arteries leading to your heart have narrowed so that not enough blood is getting through them. Cold, excessive physical exercise—even smoking—all exacerbate the problem and bring on the attacks. Going up onto the hills by yourself to bring in the ewes for lambing was nothing short of foolhardy.'

'What was I expected to do? Leave the beasts to make their own way home? Do you think I can afford to lose a whole parcel of lambs like that?' Isaac started to get up, but Elizabeth waved him back into his chair.

'I know you can't so get someone in to help you. What I'm saying, Mr Shepherd, is that you aren't fit enough to do it all yourself any longer.' Elizabeth's tone was just as determined as the old man's. 'Frank tells me that you didn't even have your medication with you when he found you this morning. At least, if you'd had the glyceryl trinitrate tablets with you, you'd have been able to control the attack.'

'For how long? Twenty...thirty minutes before it starts up again. And I'm left with a headache into the bargain.' Isaac Shepherd's tone was belligerent. 'A fine sort of medicine, I don't think!'

It was what Elizabeth had suspected. The attacks were getting stronger and more frequent from the sound of it. She chose her next words with care. 'Then I think it's time we did something more about the problem, Mr Shepherd. Obviously, the medication is no longer effective so the next logical step is to look for an alternative. I think angioplasty could be the answer.'

'What's that, Doc? An operation of some sort?' Frank enquired with interest.

'A fairly routine one nowadays. Simply explained, the section of the artery that is causing all the trouble is stretched by means of a balloon inserted into it, allowing more blood to get through to the heart. I think it would be worth considering in your father's case so I'd like to arrange for him to see a consultant at the hospital.'

'Hospital? I ain't going to no hospital!' Isaac Shepherd rose to his feet and plonked his old green cap on his head. His weathered face was flushed with temper, making Elizabeth fear that he'd set off another attack. 'It's a pity your father isn't still here, young lady. *He'd* have a sight more sense than to suggest such a thing!'

The old man stormed out of the room. Frank rose to his feet, looking more than a little embarrassed. 'I'm really sorry, Doc. Sometimes there's no point in trying to reason with him but I'll do my best, I promise you.'

'Thanks, Frank. I know how stubborn he can be, but try to make him see it's for his own good at the end of the day.'

Elizabeth smiled reassuringly, not at all put out by Isaac Shepherd's stormy exit. She was used to dealing with the sort of intransigent attitudes some of the older hill farmers had. 'Anyway, one thing I intend to do is make sure that he doesn't miss his check-ups. I'll have a word with Abbie Fraser and get her to put him on her list.'

'Rather her than me! Just warn her not to let him know when she's coming or the old devil will head for the hills!' Frank advised as he left the room.

Elizabeth laughed to herself. Isaac Shepherd was a character all right but she couldn't help admiring his gritty determination...

'Hmm, maybe I'm not the only one to get the rough edge of your tongue this morning, Dr Allen. Or do you get many of your patients storming out of your surgery like that?'

CHAPTER TWO

THE smile died on Elizabeth's lips at the sound of that surprisingly familiar deep voice. She looked up and found James Sinclair standing in the doorway, his arms folded across his chest as he regarded her with amused blue eyes.

Elizabeth felt a tingle run down her spine and shivered, although in truth she didn't feel cold. There was an odd sensation of heat seeping beneath her skin and a feeling that her heart was beating a shade faster than normal. It annoyed her almost as much as that teasing comment had done so that there was a definite snap in her voice as she replied.

'Not often, but it does happen from time to time. The patients we tend to deal with here aren't the well-heeled types you're used to, Dr Sinclair. They are too busy earning a living to waste time on the social niceties!'

'Makes them sound very grim, but that isn't the impression I got from the people I've seen this morning.' His smile widened but it held little warmth now. 'Tut-tut, *Doctor* Allen, surely you aren't trying to put me off so soon? I know we agreed on a three-month trial period but I have to confess I consider that merely a formality. I'm here to stay...believe me!'

He gave her a moment to appreciate that then glanced towards his consulting room, which was across the corridor from hers. Up until his retirement a few months earlier Elizabeth's father had used that room, and she felt a sudden pang that she hadn't moved in there herself. The thought of James Sinclair ensconced in the very room where Charles Allen had seen his patients for almost forty years suddenly stuck in her throat.

What did *he* know about all the hard work, dedication and commitment that had gone into building this practice? With his big-city attitude James Sinclair could never appreciate the community values which they all held dear. He could only ever view Yewdale as a place to work until he grew tired of playing the country GP— as he would!

He suddenly looked around and she lowered her eyes, not wanting him to see the anger she felt. It surprised her that she couldn't keep a rein on her temper, as she usually did. What was it about Sinclair that pushed all the right buttons...? Or all the wrong ones, rather? She wasn't sure but she preferred not to let him know the effect he had on her until she'd worked it out!

'Anyway, to get back to the reason I needed a word with you, Elizabeth. I've a patient in with me I'd like a second opinion on. You'll know the family, I imagine. The name's Jackson and it's the youngest child, five-year-old Chloe, who's been brought in today.'

James's voice held nothing other than professional concern now and Elizabeth gratefully latched onto it. 'Yes, I know them. They're regular visitors, especially little Chloe. She's had several bouts of chest infection recently. What's the problem today?'

'I'm not sure.' James shrugged. 'Her chest seems clear enough. I checked that straight away, after reading her notes, so I don't think that's the problem. Evidently, she's been running a fever for a few days now. And there's definite enlargement of the lymphatic glands and the spleen, which is bothering me. She also has a rash, which I'd like you to take a look at and see what you think.'

'Of course.' Elizabeth got up from her desk as James

stepped aside for her to precede him across the corridor. He reached around her to open the door and Elizabeth had to clamp down on the frisson that ran through her as his arm brushed her shoulder.

She went into the room, deliberately blanking the sensation from her mind as she saw the young woman seated in the chair with a child on her knee. The Jackson family was well known in the town, although perhaps not for the best of reasons!

Barry Jackson made regular appearances before the local magistrates for minor misdemeanours such as poaching. Rumor had it that he also wasn't averse to the odd bit of pilfering from tourists who unwisely left their cars unlocked, although he'd never been caught.

He'd go to court, pay his fines and then carry on scratching a living for himself and his family, doing odd jobs around the town. There were five Jackson children in all, ranging in age from sixteen-year-old Sophie to the youngest child, Chloe, who was huddled on her mother's knee.

'Hello, Mrs Jackson,' Elizabeth, said as she went over to them. She bent and gave the little girl a smile, noticing immediately how pale and listless the child was. 'Hello, Chloe. I believe you aren't feeling very well again?'

'She's had this fever, like I was telling Dr Sinclair here.' Annie Jackson cast a coquettish glance in James's direction as she tossed her bleached blonde hair.

'I've just been explaining all that to Dr Allen. Would you mind if she has a look at Chloe just to see what she thinks about that rash?' he said, with a charming smile that made the young woman blush.

'Course not. Here, Chloe, you stand up while the doctor takes a look at you.' Annie heaved the wan-faced little girl unceremoniously off her lap and plonked her onto her feet. She ignored the plaintive wail the child gave and turned to James with a weary sigh. 'Never stopped whining all week, she hasn't. I'm sick to death of hearing her. That's why I thought I'd bring her in today so as you can give her something to shut her up.'

'We'll see what we can do,' James replied levelly, but Elizabeth heard the edge in his voice. However, there was no sign of it as he bent over Chloe. His tone was so gentle now that the little girl stopped crying at once, looking shyly up at him through spiky wet lashes.

'How about sitting on my special couch while we look at your tummy again, Chloe? Then if you're a really good girl maybe I can find you something to take home as a reward.'

The child nodded as she slid her hand trustingly into his and let him lead her to the couch. He lifted her onto it, saying something in a low undertone that brought a hesitant smile to Chloe's face. He turned to Elizabeth, his brows rising questioningly as he realised she was still standing by the desk. 'Do you want to take a look now?'

His tone held no trace of either the annoyance she'd heard at the dismissive way Annie had treated the little girl or the gentleness with which he'd gained Chloe's trust.

Elizabeth frowned as she crossed the room, trying to equate either with the image she'd formed of James Sinclair in the weeks since she and David had interviewed him, but it was impossible. The picture she'd formed of a suave, dispassionate professional was at odds with what she'd just witnessed. It made her wonder if there might be rather more to the debonair Dr Sinclair than she'd given him credit for...

'See there...how the rash has started to change color.' James eased Chloe gently onto her side and pointed to an area just above her waist. He glanced at Elizabeth when she didn't respond. 'Elizabeth?'

'Yes, I see.' Hurriedly, Elizabeth curtailed that strange notion as she bent to study the area in question. Most of the child's trunk and limbs were covered in tiny red dots, but here she could see that their colour had deepened to a purplish hue as they'd formed larger patches.

Intrigued, she eased Chloe onto her stomach while she checked her back, and found more areas where the spots were changing colour. 'I see what you mean. A definite purpuric rash is starting to form. Some sort of acute infection possibly? Or an anaphylactic reaction to something she's eaten or come into contact with? That often results in this kind of virulent rash.'

'Hmm, I thought of that, but it doesn't explain the prolonged fever or the swelling of the lymph glands and spleen.' James sighed. 'I suppose some sort of acute infection is the most likely but I just have this gut feeling that it's more than that.'

'So what do you want to do?' Elizabeth frowned. 'A blood test?'

'I think so, don't you? We need to know what's causing the rash before we can deal with it effectively. I'd hate to think that I was cutting corners, especially on the first day of my trial.' He gave Elizabeth a teasing smile, then glanced around as Annie came over to join them.

'What do you think it is, Dr Sinclair? Nothing catching, I hope. I told Chloe's teacher that it was just a bit of a rash, like, and nothing to worry about, but she wouldn't let me take her into school.' Annie sighed heavily. 'Kids eh! Who'd have 'em? If it isn't one thing it's another, especially with this one!'

'I'm not sure exactly what it is, Mrs Jackson, which is why I'd like to do a blood test. However, I don't think that Chloe should be in school. Even if it isn't contagious, she obviously isn't feeling well.'

James's smile was cool as he moved away to collect

a sterile hypodermic syringe from the drawer. 'If you'd
sit Chloe on your knee, Mrs. Jackson, I'll just take some
blood from her arm.'

'Oh, I don't know about that, Doctor.' Annie shot a
horrified glance at the syringe. 'I never liked needles,
you see. Make me go all funny they do, just looking at
them.'

James sighed. 'Then perhaps it would be better if you
sat down and let Dr Allen and I do it.'

It took no time at all to get the sample they needed.
Chloe was as good as gold, never making a murmur as
James gently drew of a small quantity of blood.
Snapping the needle off the end of the vial, he popped
it into the sharps box then lifted the little girl from the
couch.

'I wish all my patients were as good as you, Chloe.
That was a really brave girl.' He ruffled her mousy hair
and earned himself another smile. Chloe's eyes were
adoring as they followed him across the room, making
Elizabeth smile as she pressed an adhesive dressing over
the pinprick on the child's thin arm.

It was obvious that James had a way with children,
she thought, then realised that was something else she
hadn't expected. It shook her to know that her assessment of him had been nowhere near as accurate as she'd
imagined it to be.

'Right, I'll give you a prescription for penicillin,
which Chloe must take as directed. I see that she's had
it before—there was no adverse reaction to it, Mrs
Jackson?' James asked, looking up.

'Oh, no. Cleared up her cough a treat it did. So, how
soon can I send her in to school?' Annie unceremoniously bundled the child into her coat. 'I can't get a minute's peace with her under me feet all day!'

'Keep her off until the rash goes. Until we're sure it

isn't contagious, it's only sensible,' James's tone was brusque. 'It will be a week to ten days before the results of the blood test come through. We'll give you a call as soon as we get them. In the meantime, make sure that Chloe has plenty of rest and if her temperature starts to rise again sponge her down and give her plenty to drink. If you're at all worried, though, call the surgery and I'll come out to see her.'

'Right you are, Dr Sinclair, although I still think it's a lot of fuss over nothing, keeping her off school.' Annie marched to the door, dragging the little girl with her. Chloe cast a pleading glance in James's direction, although she didn't say anything.

'Oh, just a minute, Mrs Jackson,' he called, as he suddenly got up. Elizabeth frowned, wondering what he was up to as he quickly crossed the room and bent down in front of Chloe.

'I nearly forgot, didn't I? And after I promised you a reward for being such a good girl.' He gave the child a warm smile as he straightened. 'That's for being my star patient.'

Chloe lovingly fingered the shiny silver star he'd pinned to her old anorak. 'Thank you,' she whispered shyly.

'You're welcome, Chloe.' He opened the door, responding pleasantly to Annie's goodbye. However, there was a look of exasperation on his face as he went back to his desk. 'That woman...!'

Elizabeth laughed, surprised to find herself in accord with him on one point at least. 'I know what you mean. Annie's never going to win a ''Mother of the Year'' title, is she? Still, in all fairness, she does her best and I don't doubt that in her own way she loves those children. The trouble is she was little more than a child herself when she had her first and then along came four more.'

'It's often the way. The ones least able to cope are the ones who have the most!' James laughed. He tipped back his chair and regarded her curiously. 'How about you, Elizabeth? Do you have a family? Are you married? Somehow we never got around to that at the interviews. I remember something being said about David's wife having died recently but nothing was mentioned about your own situation.'

Elizabeth shook her head, wondering why the question should make her feel so self-conscious. It was natural that James should be curious about his practice partners and yet the interest she saw in his eyes seemed to go beyond that...

She shut off that ridiculous thought, smiling coolly as she replied. 'No, I don't have any children, nor am I married.'

'Divorced, then?'

'Of course not!' It was proving difficult to maintain the cool smile but Elizabeth managed it—just.

'Then maybe you're "spoken for"?' He shot a laughing glance at her left hand yet his eyes were oddly intent when they rose to her face once more. 'No sign of a ring, I see, although a lot of people don't bother with that nowadays. Most couples I know are quite happy to live together until the urge to name the big day hits them, and then they start thinking about buying rings.'

Elizabeth took a deep breath, wondering why she was letting such nonsense disturb her. It was just the strange way that James was looking at her...as though her answer really *mattered* to him! 'I am not "spoken for". Nor am I living with anyone. I hardly think that would be appropriate behaviour for someone in my position!'

'Meaning that the good people of this town would be shocked?' James laughed softly and yet there seemed to be a trace of satisfaction in his deep voice. 'Come on,

Elizabeth. Nobody would turn a hair in this day and age!'

'Maybe not in London but things tend to be rather different around here,' she retorted tartly. 'Perhaps you should bear that in mind.'

'Oh, don't worry. I'll try not to bring the practice into disrepute with my dissolute lifestyle.' He grinned as she opened her mouth. 'Just teasing. What I'm really trying to say is that I'm surprised someone hasn't snapped you up before now.'

Her heart beat a shade faster at the compliment, although she doubted that he really meant it. Elizabeth turned and headed for the door, deciding that it was better to put an end to the conversation before it got completely out of hand. However, at that moment David suddenly appeared.

'Ah, so here you both are. I was just wondering what time you want us tonight, Liz.' He cast a glance at James.

'Liz has mentioned that we're all invited to her house tonight, I hope? We thought it would be a nice way to welcome you to your new job. It's just us three plus Sam O'Neill, who's been our locum here for the past year, and Abbie Fraser, the district nurse. Sam's in London today, being interviewed for a job overseas, but he'll be back by tonight so he'll be able to tell us how he got on. Maybe it will be a double celebration, although we'll be sorry to lose him.'

'Sounds good to me. Thanks. I'll look forward to it.' James's brows arched as he looked at Elizabeth. 'What time do you want me to be there?'

'A-around eight will be fine. It will give us all time to get straight after surgery,' she replied shortly, still unsettled by the strange conversation they'd just had. She turned to David again, her tone unconsciously softening. 'Will you be able to get a sitter for Emily? I never thought to ask before.'

'Mike said he'll do it,' David grinned so that some of the tiredness left his face. 'For a price! I believe we settled on a fiver as the going rate for looking after a kid sister!'

Elizabeth laughed at that. She glanced over her shoulder, her tone warmly amused as she explained the situation to James. 'Mike and Emily are David's children.'

'Mmm, I gathered that. But I thought you had three children, David. Did I get it wrong?'

'No, not at all,' David's face clouded over. 'Holly, my oldest daughter, is away at the moment so there's just Mike and Emily at home now.'

He gave them a quick smile but Elizabeth could see that he was upset. She sighed as he left the room, realising that she should explain the situation to James.

'Holly took her mother's death very hard. She couldn't come to terms with the fact that nothing could be done for Kate. She was at medical school in Liverpool but she dropped out after Kate died. The last I heard she was in Brazil, but I'm not sure if even David has any idea where she is at the moment.'

'Tough, both for David and his family, from the sound of it. It can't have been easy for any of them.' There was a brooding quality to James's voice which she couldn't understand. He gave her a faintly wry smile. 'It's always better to understand the situation, I find, Elizabeth. That way you don't run the risk of putting your foot in it. I think I may have been a bit slow on the uptake before, although I've no idea why you and David are so secretive.'

'Secretive?' Elizabeth repeated, wondering what on earth he was getting at.

'Mmm, about you two being an item.' He shrugged,

missing the shocked gasp she gave. 'He's a free agent now, like you. Surely the good people of Yewdale would be delighted at the thought of two of their doctors forming a different kind of partnership so that can't be the problem.'

'I...We...' Elizabeth didn't know what to say. She could feel the embarrassed heat sweeping through her whole body. Her hazel eyes were huge as they met the blue ones, which were studying her with dawning comprehension...

'Maybe I'm still not reading the situation right. Maybe David hasn't any idea how you feel about him.' He gave a chiding laugh, although there was a gleam in his eyes which she found impossible to decipher. 'You should try telling him, if you want my advice. There seems precious little point in keeping it to yourself!'

Elizabeth spun round, unable to stand there under that mocking scrutiny a moment longer. She made her way across the corridor to her own room and closed the door, thinking of all the things she should have said to let James know that she didn't appreciate either his interest or his advice! Her relationship with David wasn't any of his business.

She bit back a bitter laugh as the irony of that thought struck her. What relationship? As far as David was concerned, she was a friend and colleague, nothing more! Neither before nor after Kate's death had he given her any reason to believe otherwise. David was blissfully unaware of her feelings but it had taken James Sinclair just minutes to guess how she felt!

Elizabeth took a deep breath but it didn't help. Knowing that James could read her so easily suddenly made her feel very vulnerable indeed...

CHAPTER THREE

THERE was a list of calls to do after morning surgery, which kept Elizabeth busy for most of the afternoon. She got back just before four and hurried to the staffroom to make herself a cup of coffee before evening surgery began, stopping short when she discovered James already there.

He looked round as he heard her footsteps and smiled as he held the jar of coffee aloft. 'Want one? The kettle's just boiled.'

'Well...' Elizabeth hesitated before it struck her how ridiculous it was to refuse the offer. 'Please.'

James brought the coffee over to the table and sat down with a rueful sigh. 'My head's spinning! There's so much to take in when you start a new job, isn't there?'

Elizabeth took a quick breath as she sat down, determined not to let him see how uneasy she felt. Those comments he'd made about her and David hadn't been exactly guaranteed to make her feel comfortable around him! 'There is. It must seem a bit confusing at first, I imagine.'

'It certainly does!' James took a sip of his coffee and grimaced. 'Still, give me a week or so and I'm sure it will feel as though I've been here for ages.'

Elizabeth didn't say anything as there wasn't much she could think of which would sound sincere. She searched for something uncontroversial instead. 'Did David get a chance to go over that map of the area you'll be covering? We thought it would help if you had some idea where places are around here as that will present the biggest problem for you.'

'Think so?' There was an undercurrent to James's deep voice which brought her eyes winging to his face, although she wasn't sure she understood the expression she found there.

He shrugged as he looked down at his cup. 'You're right, I expect. Finding my way around isn't going to be easy at first, but you and David seem to have covered that.' He glanced up and this time there was no trace of anything other than gratitude in his clear blue eyes. 'That map you prepared will be a big help, though. I appreciate all the trouble you've gone to.'

'It was nothing,' Elizabeth dismissed his thanks with a quick smile. She finished her coffee then got up to wash her cup, glancing around as James came over to wash his cup as well. He reached for the teatowel as she put it down and she felt a shiver run through her as their hands touched.

She moved hurriedly out of the way and searched for something to say, aware of a sudden tension in the room although she wasn't sure what was causing it. 'We thought it would help if we marked the outlying farms on the ordnance survey map of this area. A lot of the smaller farms, in particular, are difficult to find. Unless you have some idea where you're going you can spend hours driving around, getting nowhere.'

'I can imagine.' James tossed the teatowel onto the draining-board. 'I realise that finding my way about will be a bit of a problem at first, but anyone new to the area would experience the same difficulties, I imagine. I hope I won't lose too many brownie points if I get lost a time or two.'

There was a slight edge to the teasing remark which brought a little colour to Elizabeth's cheeks. Obviously,

James was aware that she had reservations about him, working here in Yewdale, and it made her feel faintly guilty because there seemed little justification for how she felt. She gave a deprecating laugh, trying to keep the mood light.

'I'm sure you're allowed the odd slip-up so don't worry about it.' She glanced at her watch, suddenly anxious to put an end to the conversation. 'Well, I'd better get on. I need to write up some notes before surgery starts.'

She turned to leave but paused when James said softly behind her, 'I'm looking forward to working with you, Elizabeth. I think that you and I will make a great team once any initial difficulties have been ironed out.'

Elizabeth shot him a quick smile, although she didn't say anything. She went to her room and closed the door, sighing as she thought about what he'd said. Try as she may, she couldn't imagine working with James in the same degree of harmony as she did with David.

A shiver ran through her and she hastily curtailed that thought, not wanting to delve too deeply into why it worried her so much.

'Is that it, then? There's nobody else waiting?' Elizabeth took the bundle of record cards to the reception desk and handed them to Eileen, who dropped them into a tray.

'No, thank heavens. David's already gone and said to tell you that he'd see you later.' Eileen popped the cover on the computer with a sigh of relief. 'What a day! It's been non-stop ever since I got here. Mind you, having James here was a big help. We wouldn't have managed half so well—' She broke off with a laugh. 'Were your ears burning, then?'

'Why? Were you talking about me?' James demanded teasingly as he came over to the desk and gave her his batch of cards. 'I hope it was only nice things you were saying, Eileen.'

'Wouldn't you like to know?' Eileen joked as she picked up her raincoat. 'Well, I'll be off now. I'll file that little lot tomorrow. Don't forget to lock up, Elizabeth, will you?'

'I won't,' Elizabeth promised, hiding a smile. Eileen had a tendency to boss everyone around but she was so good at her job that none of them minded. She followed the older woman to the door and waited while Eileen tied a plastic rain-hood over her immaculate grey hair. After Eileen had left, Elizabeth locked the outside door, then set about switching off the lights.

'Do you switch them all off or leave some on for security reasons?' James asked as he watched her.

'We leave the one over the desk on—and that's really only in case we're called out during the night and need to come in here to get a patient's notes.' Elizabeth turned to make her way back across the darkened room and saw that James was still standing by the desk. The light from the single spotlight turned his fair hair the colour of old gold and made his tan appear even deeper.

She was suddenly conscious of how quiet it was now that everyone had gone, the muted lighting lending the room an intimate atmosphere it didn't normally possess. Shadows darkened the corners so that it seemed the room had shrunk to that one small area where James stood in the glowing pool of light. Her footsteps slowed, although she couldn't explain her reluctance to move closer and step into that circle of light.

'You said at the interview that you handle all your own night-time calls. Do you get many of them?'

His tone betrayed nothing but professional interest so Elizabeth couldn't explain the flurry which ran through her as the rich tones flowed towards her. Why should she suddenly feel so aware of the fact that they were alone? She had no idea, but she couldn't quite keep the tremor from her voice as she replied.

'It depends. You can't foretell if you're going to have a quiet evening or not, although, most people around here are very good about not calling a doctor out unnecessarily.'

Her tone was huskier than she liked so she attempted to ginger it up. 'You'll find that country people tend to be more self-reliant, especially those living some distance from the surgery.'

'Meaning that they see their doctor less often than someone living in the city might?' James shrugged. 'I suppose that has both advantages and disadvantages. OK, so you cut out a lot of time wasted on trivialities but there's always the danger that something serious might not be spotted early enough.'

It was a valid point. Making patients understand that it was vital they came into surgery to discuss any problems at an early stage was something that concerned both her and David. It surprised her, though, that James was astute enough to see that so quickly.

'You're quite right,' she admitted. 'There have been several instances when I've wished that I'd seen a patient sooner. It's something I do worry about.'

'Have you thought of setting up a monthly clinic where people could drop in for a check-up, maybe discuss any minor concerns they have? It might encourage them to come in.'

Elizabeth frowned. 'You mean along the lines of a well-woman clinic?'

'Yes, although it should be open to both men and women.' James sighed. 'There's a real need for men to start taking more of an interest in preventative medicine, I always feel.'

.

'It sounds like an excellent idea, but I'm not sure we could offer such a service,' Elizabeth explained, feeling easier now that the conversation had been confined to such relatively safe topics. 'We've been so pushed since my father retired that just getting through the everyday business of the practice has been difficult enough.'

'Maybe we need to have a rethink on how things are done?'

'What do you mean?' Elizabeth was instantly on the defensive. 'There's no way that David or I would agree to cutting corners. The service we provide here is something we're proud of!'

'I'm sure you are, but there's always room for improvement even in the best-run practice.' James nodded towards the computer. 'Taking full advantage of the latest developments in technology is one way we could offer an even better service and save time in the long run.

'A number of rural practices have realised that and installed video links to their local hospital. Patients can come into the surgery to talk with their GP *and* a consultant to decide on a course of treatment. Far too often we end up seeing a patient repeatedly because an outpatient appointment has been missed.'

'I hardly think the people around here would like that idea!' Elizabeth retorted. 'They're used to a personal service, not being diagnosed by...by remote control!'

'Obviously, it isn't suitable for every type of ailment. However, the advantages of getting a consultant's opinion on dermatological problems, for instance, must be obvious. We'd be offering patients the most up-to-date treatment available, without them having to travel further than their local surgery.'

It was a valid point but there were other considerations to be taken into account, which James hadn't allowed for because he didn't know enough about the running of the practice yet.

'I'll admit the idea is a good one,' she began.

'But?' James laughed, his blue eyes dancing with amusement. 'I get the distinct impression there's a sting in the tail of that compliment, Elizabeth.'

She didn't appreciate being teased like that. Her tone was brusque when she continued, '*But* the cost of setting up such a scheme would be extremely high, I imagine. We work to a very tight budget here, James, and I think it would take a great deal to convince David and me that such a project would be worth putting any other plans on hold for.'

'I know that finance is tight. It is in most practices these days, and that goes for city practices as well. However, we might be able to get round that by finding someone willing to sponsor us. Firms are quite keen to contribute towards projects that will enhance their standing in the local community so it's worth looking into.'

'Perhaps.' Elizabeth shrugged, still not convinced. 'But personal care is something we believe in very strongly here. It's the basis on which my father founded this practice, in fact. Technology is all well and good, and I'm sure there's a place for it—'

'Only not here in Yewdale?' James laughed softly. 'Hmm, somehow I guessed you'd say that, Elizabeth.'

She didn't like the comment, especially not in view of how easily he'd read her mind that morning! Was she really such an open book to him?

The idea was disturbing. Maybe that was why she failed to look what she was doing as she made her way quickly across the room, determined to put an end to the conversation before it went any further. Elizabeth gasped in alarm as she stepped on something which was lying

on the floor in front of the desk and was pitched off
balance.

'Careful!' James reached out and caught her as she
stumbled. He drew her to him to steady her, and
Elizabeth felt a shudder run through her as the heat from
his body seeped into hers as they came into sudden contact.

Her breath seemed to catch as she looked up and saw
the expression on his face, a mixture of concern and an
awareness that stunned her. To see James looking at her
like that was something she'd never expected and she
didn't know how to handle it.

He let her go almost immediately and bent to pick up
the offending object, which turned out to be a Lego
building block. He tossed it into the bucket of blocks on
the table where the children's toys were kept. When he
turned to her again there was no trace of anything other
than wry amusement on his face. 'Just what you need to
round off the day, isn't it—a sprained ankle?'

'I'm fine, really.' Her voice sounded strained in con-
trast to the evenness of his. She cleared her throat, wondering if it had been the subdued lighting which had put
that odd expression on his face just now.

She turned away, wanting to believe it because anything else was too disturbing to contemplate. 'Anyway,
I'd better get through to the house. Mrs Lewis will be
wondering where I've got to.'

'That's your housekeeper, isn't it?' James followed
her into the corridor, waiting while she bolted the door.

'That's right. She's been with us for years—since my
mother died, in fact. I don't know how Daddy would
have coped with Jane and me if she hadn't been around.
Mrs Lewis virtually brought us up.'

'Jane?' James leant against the wall, listening to what
she was saying with evident interest. It served to make

Elizabeth even more self-conscious so that she was all fingers and thumbs as she struggled with the bolt. It was always stiff but she couldn't recall having this much trouble with it before.

'Here, let me do that.' James brushed her hand aside and shot the bolt home. Elizabeth stepped back, feeling the jolt of heat that raced through her again from the point where their hands had met. She saw James cast her a curious look and struggled to find something to say to stop him wondering what was wrong with her, although how she could explain the strange way she was behaving she had no idea!

'Jane is my sister. She's three years older than me. She lives in Australia, just outside Perth, with her husband and three children. Brian is a consultant at the hospital there.' Elizabeth knew she was gabbling but she couldn't seem to stop the fast flow of words. 'My father has gone out there to stay with Jane for a few months while he recuperates from the heart attack he had just after Christmas.'

'Oh, yes, I heard all about that.' James laughed softly as he saw her surprise. 'Several of the patients I saw today were at pains to tell me all about Dr Charles. I got the impression they were making sure I knew I'd have a hard job, living up to his standards!'

Elizabeth laughed with him, feeling a little more at ease now they were on safe ground. 'My father is very highly thought of in Yewdale. I doubt anyone will ever match him in the town's affections.'

'Oh, I don't know about that, Elizabeth. From the comments I heard today, most people in this town hold you in very high regard.'

Elizabeth didn't know what to say in answer to the softly voiced compliment. There had been no hint of mockery in James's voice, just a deep sincerity and unstinting generosity which she hadn't expected. She'd had him down as someone who'd be very competitive in his own field, not given to complimenting others...

She took a quick breath, realising that the silence was running on a shade too long, although James didn't appear at all uncomfortable. He was watching her with a smile that made her wonder if he knew how mixed up she was feeling! The thought was just the catalyst she needed.

'Well, that's good to hear. I'd better go through to the house. I...I'll see you later, I expect.'

'I'm looking forward to it, Elizabeth.'

There was a lingering warmth in his deep voice, which Elizabeth tried hard to ignore. She didn't look back as she made her way along the corridor and quickly let herself into the house. The surgery had been built onto the side of Yewdale House and many times she'd been grateful for the convenience of not having to spend time travelling to work. Now, however, she experienced a momentary qualm.

Knowing that James Sinclair was within calling distance for the best part of each day was strangely unsettling, even though she had no idea why it should be.

'Crackers and cheese! Why, I've never heard the like. What would your father say, Miss Elizabeth?'

'It's just a quick get-together, Mrs Lewis, to welcome Dr Sinclair to his new job. You always go to your sister's on Mondays so I didn't want to trouble you,' Elizabeth explained, but she knew her words were falling on deaf ears. Mrs Lewis had already made up her mind and that was that!

'And a fine welcome it would be, offering the poor man crackers and cheese!' Mrs Lewis drew herself up to her full five feet and sniffed. 'It's a good job Dr Ross

happened to mention what was going on when I saw
him this morning. I came home early from Agnes's so
I had chance to put a little something together.'

Without giving Elizabeth time to say anything more,
she led the way into the dining-room. 'I've made a buffet—nothing fancy, mind, just good plain food—so I
hope that Dr Sinclair likes it. One of my lamb casseroles
and a ham-and-leek pie, with salad and some home-
made rolls. Then there's rhubarb crumble to follow, with
custard, of course. Might be spring but it's a cold night
what with all that rain. I'm sure everyone will be glad
of something hot to keep out the chill.'

Elizabeth bit back a sigh as she saw the laden table.
Mrs Lewis had laid it with one of the beautiful old dam-
ask cloths and the best china. There were two huge
dishes of fragrant lamb casserole, being kept hot on
burners, beside a basket of crusty rolls and a big dish of
creamy butter. Then there was the pie with its light-as-
air crust, already cut into thick wedges and looking
mouth-wateringly tempting. Salad was piled into a big
wooden bowl next to it, a feast for the eyes as well as
the palate.

'It all looks lovely, Mrs Lewis,' Elizabeth said faintly,
'but there really was no need for you to go to so much
trouble.'

'It wasn't a bit of trouble. Now, I'll just go and check
on the crumble. We don't want it burning, do we?' Mrs
Lewis cast a last satisfied glance at the table then went
back to the kitchen. Elizabeth sighed again, knowing
when she was beaten. So much for keeping tonight's
little gathering brief!

She went to the sideboard and took out two bottles of
wine, then set about finding the corkscrew. It wasn't in
any of the drawers so she headed for the kitchen to see
if it was there. She was just crossing the hall when the

doorbell rang so she veered off to answer it, checking her watch as she did so. It wasn't eight yet but maybe David had come early.

Elizabeth cast a quick glance in the hall mirror as she passed it, smoothing a wayward strand of hair back from her face. It needed cutting, she decided critically. It had been ages since she'd had chance to get to the hairdresser's and the springy auburn waves were starting to curl around her face as though they had a life of their own.

She tucked it behind her ears then glanced down at the jade-green dress she'd decided to wear that night. It was one of her favourites, its simple lines making the most of her slender figure and elegant legs. She'd pinned a delicate gold filigree brooch to the shoulder and wore matching gold earrings as well. Suddenly she found herself wondering why she'd gone to so much trouble. She always dressed neatly but tonight she'd felt like making a special effort, even slipping on a pair of high-heeled black sandals which rarely saw the light of day.

Had it been for David's benefit that she'd decided to dress up tonight? she mused. So that he might see her in a fresh light at last? Or did the fact that James Sinclair would be here have something to do with it?

The bell rang a second time, mercifully giving her an excuse not to work out the answer to that question. Elizabeth hurried to the door and felt the welcoming smile freeze on her lips as she found not David but James on the step.

'I'm not too early, I hope?' he asked, as she stared at him, without saying a word. He gave a self-deprecating laugh when she still didn't speak. 'I wasn't sure how long it would take to walk here from the pub so that's my excuse.'

'It...it doesn't matter.' Elizabeth took a quick breath

as she stepped aside, aware that her heart was beating rather faster than usual. 'Come in. I see it's still raining,' she added, latching onto the first thing that came to mind to make up for her initial silence. 'Here let me take your coat.'

'Thanks.' James handed it to her then stood, looking around with interest. 'Lovely house, Elizabeth, loads of character.'

'Thank you.' She hung his wet coat on the hallstand and glanced around the hall. It had been years since the house had been decorated last but that didn't detract from its innate charm, she thought. The hall still looked warmly welcoming on a night like this, with its gleaming parquet floor and faded old rugs scattered around.

She'd picked a huge armful of lilac from the garden the day before and had stuck it into a big brass jug on the hall table. Now its scent perfumed the air, mingling pleasantly with the smell of beeswax polish.

Looking around, Elizabeth decided that James was right. The house did have loads of character even if it was sorely in need of redecorating. It surprised her that he should appreciate that. She'd have imagined he would prefer some place far more ostentatious, but there was no denying the genuine admiration she saw on his face.

Once again the thought that she might have misjudged him was unsettling so she didn't say anything more as she led the way to the sitting-room, where a fire was burning in the grate to ward off the damp chill of the night.

'Have you lived here all your life, then?' James asked, as he followed her into the room.

'Yes. I was born here. Upstairs in the front bedroom, in fact. Now, what would you like to drink?' Elizabeth went to the sideboard and sorted through the bottles lined up on the old silver tray. It was disconcerting to

have to keep adjusting her mental image of him like this
when she'd been so sure that she'd had him summed up
perfectly!

'Sherry, whisky, gin,' she offered, glancing over her
shoulder and trying her best not to notice how handsome
he looked, but it was impossible to ignore it. He was
wearing brown cord trousers, which were moulded to his
long legs, and a creamy cashmere sweater that emphasised the width of his shoulders.

Elizabeth felt her senses stir in a way she couldn't
recall them ever having done before, and quickly turned
away before he noticed anything amiss. Opening the
cupboard, she pulled out a rather dusty bottle. 'There's
brandy as well if you'd prefer that.'

'Actually, tonic water would be great if you've got
it,' James said with a laugh as he sat on the sofa and
crossed his long legs. 'I'm not much of a drinker, to be
honest. The odd glass of wine with a meal and that's
about it.'

'Of course. Oh, I'll just get some ice. I forgot all about
it before.' Grateful for the excuse to leave the room,
Elizabeth hurried to the kitchen and took a tray of ice-
cubes out of the freezer. Mrs Lewis was nowhere about
so she went to the window and stood, staring out across
the rain-swept garden, while she caught her breath.

What was it about James which threw her into such a
spin? she wondered. Since the moment he'd walked into
her room that morning she hadn't known if she was on
her head or her heels half the time! Why did she react
this way around him? She couldn't recall ever having
felt like this around David...

Especially not around David! she amended hastily.
David always had a soothing influence on her, his ability
to smooth over any problems one of the things she loved
most about him.

It had been David who'd helped her through that painful period after her one and only love affair had gone so drastically wrong. She'd been in her last year at medical school and had come home one weekend and poured out the whole story to his sympathetic ears. It had been a while before she'd realised how she felt about David, although she'd taken care never to let him suspect it, yet not once in all this time could she recall being so...so *aware* of him as she was of James Sinclair!

'Here you are. I thought you must have gone to the North Pole for that ice!' The teasing note in that deep voice brought Elizabeth's eyes swinging upwards. The darkened glass acted like a mirror so that she could see James reflected in it. She felt her pulse leap as she watched him walk towards her.

He stopped and gave her a quizzical smile in the glass. 'Want me to take those?'

'I'm sorry...?' She jumped when he reached out and lifted the tray from her hand. His eyes were wryly amused as he glanced at the melting ice-cubes.

'I think these are just about past their sell-by date, don't you? Have you any more?'

'I... Yes. Yes, of course.' Elizabeth hurried to the freezer and lifted out another tray of ice-cubes, handing it to him just as the bell rang again. 'That must be the others. I...I'll go and let them in.'

She hurried from the kitchen, struggling to get a grip on herself as she crossed the hall. It wasn't easy. Her heart was beating too fast, her breathing was too rapid and a feeling of nervous excitement made her body tingle...

She took a huge breath then let it out slowly. Cool, calm and composed... It had never seemed harder to achieve a single one of those!

CHAPTER FOUR

'So, I START the beginning of October. I fly out to Mozambique and spend the first two weeks there, training, then go to one of the outlying settlements.' Sam O'Neill grinned as he helped himself to another dish of rhubarb crumble and topped it off with a swirl of creamy yellow custard. 'Think I can pack you in my suitcase, Mrs Lewis? The thought of not tasting your food for two whole years…!'

'Get along with you, Dr O'Neill!' Mrs Lewis chided, but she looked pleased all the same. 'Now, there's plenty more crumble in the kitchen if you want it. And there's coffee in the pot so help yourselves.'

'Thank you, Mrs Lewis.' Elizabeth smiled as the housekeeper left the room. She glanced around as Abbie Fraser came and flopped beside her on the sofa with a groan of relief. 'Busy day?'

'Too right!' Abbie eased off her shoes. 'I did twelve calls today. And there are at least ten already booked for tomorrow, plus anything urgent which comes in. Who'd be a district nurse?'

'You know you love the job,' David said with a smile as he came over to join them.

'True, but that doesn't mean I can't have a moan from time to time, does it?' Abbie's pretty face filled with laughter as she glanced at Sam. 'Not all of us can go swanning off to London for interviews. Some of us have to stay here and work!'

'I'll have you know I never stopped from the time I got there to the minute I got back on the train.' Sam put

40

down his dish and groaned. 'Gosh, I'm full. I didn't have time for more than a sandwich but I've certainly made up for it tonight.' He turned to James with a grin. 'There are definite advantages to being a bachelor around here. Number one on the list is that Mrs Lewis bullies Liz into inviting you around to dinner on a regular basis.'

'Sounds good to me if tonight's meal is anything to go by.' James put his own plate down. 'What made you decide to go overseas, then?'

'It's something I've always wanted to do.' Sam shrugged. 'I came here as a locum but, with one thing and another, stayed longer than any of us expected. I've enjoyed it tremendously but I don't want to end up regretting not doing what I intended to. Anyway, what made you decide to come to this area? It must be a big change after London.'

'It is.' James shrugged as he went to the fireplace and rested his arm along the mantelpiece. 'I always intended to go into private practice, to be honest, and I was actually offered a position in Harley Street a couple of months ago.'

Sam whistled softly. 'Really? What made you turn it down?'

'I realised that it wasn't what I wanted.' James's voice was reflective. Elizabeth found her eyes drawn to him. He suddenly looked up and she found her gaze held by the burning blue intensity of his as he added just as softly, 'I think I've found what I'm looking for here, though.'

'Well, we're certainly glad to have you on board. Since Charles had to retire we've been under a lot of pressure. With seven thousand patients on our books and over four hundred square miles to cover, we've been struggling recently.' David glanced at his watch then stood up. 'I'll have to go, Liz. It's been lovely, but I don't like to leave the kids on their own too long. You never know what they'll get up to! I'm on call tonight as well, but hopefully it will be quiet.'

'Of course.' Elizabeth dragged her gaze away from James, shaken by the way he'd looked at her. Maybe it was her imagination but it had seemed as though he'd been directing that comment at her...

She pushed the thought aside as David's mobile phone suddenly rang, bringing forth a wry groan from him before he answered it. He sighed as he finished the call and slipped the phone back into his pocket. 'I spoke too soon. That was Harvey Walsh over at Yewthwaite Farm. His wife has taken a tumble down the stairs and hurt her ankle. I'd better get over there right away.'

'Poor woman. Do you want me to phone Mike and let him know where you are?' Elizabeth offered, as she walked him to the door.

'Please. Tell him I'll be back as soon as I can.' David waved as he climbed into his car and drove off.

Elizabeth closed the door and went back into the hall, smiling as she found Abbie and Sam already putting on their coats. 'Are you both off as well?'

'Yes, I'm bushed, to tell the truth.' Sam grimaced. 'All I want now I've been fed is to go to bed and sleep for the next twelve hours solid!'

'Uh-oh, sounds like old age is catching up with our dashing Dr O'Neill!' Abbie teased, zipping up her quilted jacket.

'Well, you should recognise the signs. Isn't it your birthday soon? How old are you, then—forty-five?' Sam shot back, and ducked as Abbie aimed a good-natured punch at him.

'Cheeky thing! I'll be thirty-two, for your information. When did you say you were starting your new job? October? Can't come soon enough is all I can say!'

Abbie and Sam were still squabbling as they left the house. Elizabeth waved them off then returned inside again to find James, taking his coat from the hallstand.

'I think I'd better be on my way as well. I wouldn't like to outstay my welcome,' he said softly.

Elizabeth struggled to find something to say but mercifully the phone rang just then, cutting short the need to come up with some polite reply. She went to answer it, aware that James was waiting by the door.

'Yewdale Surgery, Dr Allen speaking.' She paused, listening intently as the caller identified himself as being from the ambulance control centre. Picking up a pen, she jotted down the information as he gave it to her. 'A motorbike. The rider and passenger. Right. Anyone else involved? Not so far as you know.'

James had crossed the hall to stand beside her, and she felt a frisson run through her as she caught the tangy scent of the soap he'd used that night. Suddenly she was overwhelmingly conscious of his nearness so that it was a relief to focus on essentials as the control centre asked how long it would take her to reach the emergency site.

'I should be there in about fifteen minutes, with a bit of luck. Let the paramedics know I'm on my way, will you?'

'Accident?' James asked, when she'd hung up.

'Yes. A motorbike has run off the road about ten miles the other side of town. There are two people injured, the rider and his pillion passenger. A local farmer rang the emergency services, but it will take at least forty minutes before an ambulance can get there.'

Even as she was explaining the situation Elizabeth was already moving away to unhook her coat from the stand. She shot a glance at her dress and sighed as she realised there was no time to change.

'So that's why you were called?' James queried

thoughtfully. 'Because you can get there sooner than the ambulance can?'

'Yes.' Elizabeth picked up her case. 'We cover any emergency calls within our area if we can get there faster than the ambulance, which is usually the case.'

James opened the door. 'One of the drawbacks of being so far away from a city, I suppose—takes extra time for the emergency services to reach a call?'

'That's right. The so-called "golden hour" is crucial, as you know. Those first sixty minutes after an accident are critical in determining the outcome—often the dividing line between life and death. When an ambulance has to spend most of that time just getting to a patient the chances of survival are cut right down.' Elizabeth glanced around as Mrs Lewis appeared.

'I'm going out on an emergency call, Mrs Lewis. Dr Ross is also out on a call so could you ring his house and let his son know that he'll be back as soon as he can, please?'

'Of course. Take care, now, both of you. Nasty night it is to go driving round the countryside.' Mrs Lewis shuddered as she came to the door and peered out.

'We'll be fine, Mrs Lewis. Ready?' James turned to Elizabeth, seemingly oblivious to her surprise.

'Ready?' she repeated blankly.

'Yes. Have we got everything we'll need? We'll have to take your car, I'm afraid, as I didn't come in mine.' He went out to the car and opened the door for her.

'You don't need to come!' Elizabeth fought to keep her voice level but she wasn't sure she'd be wholly successful as she saw James frown.

'Of course I do. There are two people hurt, Elizabeth. You can only deal with them one at a time. This way they'll both have the best chance possible. Now, shall we get off?'

His tone made her flush as she realised she was wasting valuable seconds, debating the point. Elizabeth hurriedly started the car as James climbed in beside her. She took a deep breath as she headed out of the drive, forcing herself to concentrate on making up for those few lost seconds. That was all she must think about now, getting to the accident as fast as possible. It was better than thinking about the man sitting beside her...far, far better!

'How much further now? We must have been driving for almost fifteen minutes, by my estimation.'

Elizabeth didn't look at him—she was too busy, concentrating on the road ahead. The rain had stopped now but the night was pitch black, making driving along the narrow unlit road hazardous. 'Not far, I expect... Look, there they are.'

She slowed the car to a crawl as she saw lights up ahead. Easing into the side of the road, she switched off the engine and wound down the window as a man came hurrying over to the car.

'Am I glad to see you, Dr Allen! I was beginning to wonder if I should go back and ring for the ambulance again.'

'It's on its way, Fred. The control centre asked me to come along and see what I can do until it gets here.' Elizabeth opened her door, grimacing as she stepped into a puddle of water. She made her way to the back of the car and took her wellingtons from the boot, swiftly exchanging the sandals for them—not the perfect accessory to the elegant dress but far more practical!

She glanced at James as he came to join them. 'Fred, this is Dr Sinclair, our new partner in the practice.'

'I heard there was someone new starting. Pleased to

meet you, Dr Sinclair. The name's Fred Murray. I live at Boundary Farm just down the road aways.'

'Nice to meet you, Fred. I'm only sorry it has to be under these circumstances, though.' James turned to Elizabeth. 'I'll go and take a look at what we have.'

'You'd better take this with you.' Elizabeth handed him the spare bag she always kept in the car for emergencies. 'There's all the usual things in it—cervical collar, pethidine and so on. I've also got a supply of saline if we need it.'

'Good.' James didn't say anything more as he headed straight to where the motorcyclist was lying beside the road. Lifting her own case from the car, Elizabeth hurriedly followed him and nodded to Fred's grandson, Billy, who was kneeling next to the young woman pillion passenger. Billy had taken off his jacket to cover her and his face looked pinched with cold as Elizabeth crouched down beside him.

'Hello, Billy. Has she come round since you got here?' she asked quietly, as she began to examine the girl.

'No. She hasn't even moved but she's breathing OK. I checked that, Dr. Allen. Grandpa wanted to take her helmet off but I told him we shouldn't do that. I saw it on a programme on the telly, you see,' he added, by way of explanation.

'Well done.' Elizabeth gave him a warm smile. 'The worst thing you can do is remove a crash helmet from a motorcyclist because of the damage it could cause to the spinal cord if the neck has been fractured. As long as the person's breathing, leave well alone until medical help arrives.'

Billy looked pleased to be told that he'd done the right thing. He followed instructions carefully and helped as Elizabeth fitted a cervical support collar around the girl's neck, before easing off her helmet. She was unconscious but breathing steadily, as Billy had said, and her colour wasn't too bad.

Elizabeth methodically checked her skull, feeling for any lumps or depressions with her fingertips. Head injuries were one of the commonest causes of death in motorbike accidents, and it was essential that she assessed the situation first.

There was no obvious damage to the skull but Elizabeth knew that there still could be damage to the brain, resulting from the fall. She raised the girl's eyelids and found that both pupils dilated evenly when she shone a small light into them, which was an encouraging sign. Unevenly dilating pupils were an indication that there was pressure building up on the brain from internal bleeding, which could have disastrous consequences.

'Did you see what happened?' Elizabeth asked as she carried on with her examination, gently sliding her hand beneath the girl's back to check for spinal damage. It was difficult to be certain because of the thick leather jacket and trousers the girl was wearing, but Elizabeth couldn't detect any obvious damage to the vertebrae.

'No. We were just driving home when we heard the crash, but by the time Grandpa and I got here it was all over and done with.' Billy pointed to where a section of the wall had been sheered away. 'Their bike's down there. They must have taken the bend too fast and skidded, with it being wet.'

'Probably. These roads are dangerous at the best of times, and on a night like this, well, you can see the results for yourself.' Elizabeth turned her attention to the girl's arms and legs next, grimacing as she found a jagged tear in the sleeve of the jacket just above the girl's elbow and felt the stickiness of blood seeping through it.

'Shine that torch here, will you, Billy? Hmm, that cut looks nasty. She must have done it when she slid along the road. Her elbow might be fractured as well, from the look of it...'

Elizabeth looked around at the sound of voices being raised. The young man who'd been steering the motorbike was struggling frantically to get up. It took both James and Fred Murray all their time to restrain him. Just when it appeared they'd succeeded he suddenly clutched his chest and collapsed.

Elizabeth scrambled to her feet, shooting out a rapid stream of instructions at young Billy. 'Run to my car and get the big case out of the boot and bring it back here—fast.'

Leaving the girl, who didn't appear to be in any immediate danger, she hurried over to James and crouched beside him. 'What's happened?'

'Left lung's collapsed,' he bit out succinctly. 'He must have hit the wall when he came off the bike. Heaven knows how many ribs he's broken—damn!' James swore softly as bloodstained froth started seeping from the corner of the man's mouth. 'A rib must have pierced the lung, from the look of it. How long is that ambulance going to be, do you think?'

'It's hard to tell. They won't be able to travel very fast with the state of these roads tonight. It could be another ten, fifteen minutes yet, and then they still have to get him back to the hospital after that,' Elizabeth replied tersely, watching the young man struggling for breath. He was very pale now, his lips already blue-tinged because insufficient oxygen was being absorbed into his bloodstream. It was obvious that something had to be done to alleviate the problem as soon as possible.

At that moment Billy arrived with the case. 'Put it down there, Billy. Thanks.' She unclipped the locks then turned to James. 'I think we need to put in a chest drain, don't you? That will release the pressure and help his lung reinflate.'

'It would. But should we attempt it here?' James frowned in concern as he took in their surroundings.

'It isn't the ideal place, I agree, but I don't think we can afford to wait for the ambulance to arrive,' she replied levelly, taking what they needed from the emergency supplies.

James shot another look at the patient then nodded, obviously convinced. 'You're right. We daren't wait and run the risk of him asphyxiating.'

Rapidly he undid the young man's jacket and shirt, before taking the chest drain from her with a wry smile. 'The last time I dealt with a haemothorax it was in the luxury of one of the world's most renowned teaching hospitals. A case of going from one extreme to another, wouldn't you say?'

Elizabeth couldn't help smiling at the dry statement. She watched as he expertly slid the drain into place, despite the less than perfect conditions under which he was working. It was proof of his skill, she thought, but, then, that had never been in any doubt. Any concerns she'd had about James had had little to do with his medical expertise!

'That should do it.' He sounded satisfied when the young man started to breathe more easily as bloody fluid escaped from the pleural cavity through the drain. He slipped an oxygen mask over the patient's nose and mouth, then glanced at Elizabeth as he began to set up a drip. 'All in all, I'd say he's been extremely lucky— fractured ribs, a possible displaced cartilage of the knee. It could have been a lot worse. How's the girl?'

'Not too bad, considering. I think she's got a fractured elbow and a nasty cut. There's always the possibility of concussion, although thankfully there doesn't seem to be any sign of a serious head injury. As you say, they seem to have got off pretty lightly.'

Elizabeth gave James a last smile before she went back to the girl. Once she'd cut through the jacket sleeve, and could see it clearly, the wound on the girl's arm proved to be less severe than she'd feared. Gentle pressure soon stopped the bleeding so that the wound could be covered with a sterile dressing, and then she set about dealing with the elbow fracture.

With Billy's help, Elizabeth arranged a thick layer of padding down the girl's side. Carefully she strapped the girl's injured arm to her body to immobilise it and prevent any damage to the underlying blood vessels and nerves. She'd just finished when the girl started to gain consciousness.

'What happened...?' she asked dazedly.

'You had an accident.' Elizabeth laid a soothing hand on her shoulder as she tried to sit up. 'Now, I want you to lie still and not try to move.'

'An accident...?' The girl frowned as she tried to make sense of what she was hearing. She suddenly gasped. 'Geoff! Is he all right? Where is he? He isn't...?'

'He's fine. He's right over there with Dr Sinclair. And I'm Dr Allen, by the way. Can you tell me your name?' Elizabeth asked, wanting to reassure herself that the girl hadn't suffered any loss of memory.

'Heather. Heather...Cargill.'

Elizabeth frowned as Heather stumbled over her last name. Maybe she'd been too optimistic if the patient was having difficulty in recalling her own name. She fixed a smile to her face, not wanting to alarm Heather by making her think something was wrong.

'And can you remember what happened, Heather? Dr Sinclair and I were asked to come here by the ambulance control centre so we have no idea what actually went on tonight.'

'I'm not sure…' Heather frowned. It was obvious she was having trouble taking everything in. 'I can remember us driving through all that rain…and Geoff turning round to tell me that it wasn't far now. Then…then we just seemed to spin out of control.' She gave a choked laugh as tears slid from her eyes. 'We got married today, too. That's why we're here—on our honeymoon. What a thing to happen!'

That explained it. No wonder Heather had had trouble recalling her new name! Elizabeth laughed in relief. 'It could have been a lot worse. At least you and Geoff are all right. He's got some broken ribs, plus a lot of bruises, and I rather think that your elbow is fractured, but there's nothing that won't heal.' She heard the wail of a siren in the distance. 'And it sounds as though the ambulance has made it at last. It won't be long before you're safely tucked up in a hospital bed.'

The girl managed a wry smile. 'It wasn't quite what we had in mind!'

It took another twenty minutes or so after the ambulance arrived to get the young couple on board. Elizabeth watched the ambulance drive off into the night and sighed ruefully. 'What a start to married life!'

James laughed as he began to pack everything away. 'I don't imagine the honeymoon is going to be quite what they'd envisaged! Still, it'll be something to tell their grandchildren about in years to come.'

Elizabeth laughed softly, amused by that thought. 'I suppose that's one way to look at it.' Fred and Billy came to join them. 'Thanks a lot for all your help tonight, you two. You were brilliant. We couldn't have managed half so well without you.'

'Oh, don't mention it, Dr Allen. Glad we could help.

And even more pleased that it turned out all right at the end of the day.' Fred and Billy waved goodbye as they climbed into Fred's old Land Rover and roared off in a cloud of fumes.

'Well, that's that. Time we got back ourselves.' James lifted the case into the back of the car then ran a hand through his dishevelled fair hair. 'I must say it's been an exciting start to my tenure here. And to think that people tried to tell me that rural practice would be boring!' He grinned as he slammed the boot. 'I'm glad I didn't listen!'

'Why didn't you?' Elizabeth frowned as she got into the car. 'You told Sam tonight that you'd been offered a position in Harley Street so why did you turn it down to come to Yewdale?' She gave a soft laugh, unaware of the challenge it held.

'Believe me, there are going to be a lot of days which are short on excitement. Wait until you have to drive for two hours on a night call to get to one of the outlying farms, and then have to drive all the way back. You could find yourself regretting your decision to leave the bright city lights behind!'

'Think so? But, then, you don't have any idea how much thought I gave this. It wasn't just some spur-of-the-moment decision, Elizabeth. I thought about it long and hard before I made up my mind,' he replied evenly.

Elizabeth turned the car and headed back towards the town. 'You may think you've considered every aspect of the job, but working in a practice like this is very different from what you're used to. Even you admitted that this afternoon. I don't think anyone can fully appreciate what the job entails until they've experienced the highs and lows for themselves.'

'And you think that once I've experienced them then I'll regret my decision to come here. Is that why you're so hostile towards me? Maybe we're getting to the truth at last.' James turned to look at her, his handsome face set into such grim lines that Elizabeth felt a frisson run down her spine.

She shrugged, knowing she should deny the accusation but unable to bring herself to do so. Perhaps 'hostile' wasn't the word she'd have used but it would do.

'Feeling like that, why did you agree to offer me the partnership in the first place? You had your chance to turn me down after the interviews, Elizabeth. Why didn't you do so then?' His voice was hard-edged, like steel beneath velvet, but beneath the anger she sensed a measure of hurt.

It disturbed her in a way she wouldn't have expected it to. So what if James was hurt by her attitude—what did it matter? But it did, and the realisation stung so much that she didn't attempt to soften her reply.

'You were the best qualified—on paper, at least.' She didn't look at him, concentrating on the road as they crested the hill. The moon had come out at last and in the valley below she could see Yewdale, lying serenely in the silvery light. It was a picture of peace that contrasted sharply with the maelstrom of emotions she felt at that moment.

'Damned by faint praise, indeed!' James's tone was biting as he leaned over and switched off the ignition so that Elizabeth was forced to bring the car to a stop at the side of the road.

'Do you mind?' She turned to glare at him, feeling her heart jolt as she saw the expression in his eyes. There was anger there, as she might have expected, but once again there was that suggestion of hurt, which disturbed her so.

She took a quick breath to iron any trace of uncertainty from her voice. 'What on earth do you think you're doing?'

'Getting this sorted out once and for all, that's what.' His hand closed over hers as she went to restart the engine. His face was all angles in the silvery light as he bent towards her, his eyes leached of colour so that they seemed to shimmer like molten silver. The very air seemed to vibrate with tension and Elizabeth found herself holding her breath, only letting it out when James abruptly sat back in his seat.

'We need to talk and I prefer to do it here where nobody but us can hear what's said.'

'I can't see what there is to talk about!' she retorted sharply, shaken by what had happened. She ran a hand over her hair and felt it tremble, and was shocked. Why did it feel as though for a moment there she'd been poised on the brink of something dangerous, something that had the power to turn her world upside down? She had no idea, but it was hard to shrug off the feeling.

'Because you've already made up your mind, and nothing is going to change it?' James laughed shortly, gaining her immediate attention. She cast him a wary look but he was staring straight ahead, not at her. He suddenly turned to look at her and she felt her heart give that odd little jolt once more as his eyes blazed into hers, full of anger and hurt and so many other things that she couldn't understand half of what she saw in them. It was only when he turned away again with a sigh that she was able to think straight.

'Look, James, this is pointless—' she began, but he cut her off as though he hadn't even heard her.

'I wonder if it would help if you knew exactly what I gave up to come here, Elizabeth. Perhaps that will convince you that this wasn't some hasty decision.'

Elizabeth took a quick breath, wishing she'd never

started this. If she'd had doubts she should have kept them to herself rather than promote this kind of discussion, yet pride refused to let her back down.

'I'm going to take an awful lot of convincing, James. All right, maybe you do think this is the right job for you, but for how long? A month? Six? Maybe a year at most? And then what happens? Will you realise that the life of a country GP is a world away from the idyllic existence portrayed in all those television programmes?'

'My, my, you really do have a high opinion of me, don't you, Elizabeth?' He gave the softest laugh imaginable. Elizabeth couldn't for the life of her understand why it made her feel so nervous. Her hands clenched on the steering-wheel as he continued in that same deceptively mild tone.

'I hate to disillusion you but I didn't apply for this post because I was looking for an ''idyllic'' lifestyle. On the contrary, I wanted this job because I felt I could make a valuable contribution to the work you do here. I was also attracted by the idea of becoming part of the local community, believe it or not.' He paused, choosing his words with care.

'For years I'd believed that what I wanted was to go into private practice, but when the opportunity arose I realised I'd simply been doing what was expected of me.'

'Expected? By whom?' Despite herself, Elizabeth was intrigued.

'By my parents, to begin with.' He sighed as he leaned back against the headrest. 'My father was a leading orthopaedic consultant before he retired. He expected a great deal of me—rightly so, as I was given every advantage from an early age. He accepted my decision to become a GP because he assumed I'd go into private practice one day.'

'I take it that he doesn't approve of your decision to come here?' Elizabeth queried, noting the wry note in his voice.

'Not really. I don't think either my mother or my father understands it.' He gave her a thin smile but his eyes were hooded so that it was impossible to tell what he was thinking. 'However, they weren't the only ones to find it hard to accept that this was what I want to do with my life. Harriet made no bones about the fact she thought I was mad to turn down the Harley Street offer.'

'Harriet?' The question came out before she could stop it, and Elizabeth regretted it immediately. James's private life wasn't any of her concern. Yet she couldn't deny that she was intensely curious to know who this woman was.

'Harriet Carr. We lived together for almost two years.' He shrugged. 'We might even have ended up getting married if I hadn't decided that I wanted this job.'

'You mean that she…refused to come with you to Yewdale?' Elizabeth heard the surprise in her voice, but it was only when James laughed that she realised what interpretation he might have put on it. She was glad of the darkness as she felt the colour run up her face. She'd made it sound as though she couldn't imagine why any woman would refuse to accompany him to the ends of the earth!

'Unfortunately, Harriet couldn't imagine living anywhere but London. She refused to consider moving here, even if it meant we'd be together.' James's voice was smoky with amusement. Elizabeth felt her embarrassment rise another notch up the scale as she realised he *had* put that very connotation on her words.

She avoided looking at him as he continued levelly, 'I don't think Harriet believed I would actually go through with it, to be honest. She probably expected me to change my mind once I knew how against the idea she was.'

He shrugged again, his shoulder brushing Elizabeth's in the confined space so that she felt a flutter run through her—a flash of instant awareness that seemed to make her blood heat a degree or two hotter.

'But you didn't change your mind, obviously.' Elizabeth's own voice was faintly husky now, and she hastily cleared her throat as she saw him glance at her. 'Didn't you try to explain your reasons for wanting to work here, James?'

'Oh, yes. I spent hours, trying to make Harriet understand that it was something I not only wanted to do but *needed* to do. Unfortunately, she had just as much trouble understanding my motives as you apparently have, Elizabeth. Maybe I can understand Harriet's attitude in a way, but I can't understand yours.'

His eyes locked on her face, and she saw the burning light of conviction that shone in them. 'I intend to do a good job here. I promise you that. I know how much this community means to you and how committed you are to serving its needs. All I ask is that you give me the chance to prove my worth.'

She didn't know what to say. Faced with his obvious sincerity, it seemed harsh to repeat her doubts, but what he'd told her had done little to set her mind at rest. If anything, it had given her more reason to worry!

What would happen if James decided that he missed Harriet too much to remain apart from her? Faced with Harriet's intransigence, what choice would he have but to return to London? Ultimately it could all boil down to one simple question—how much did he love Harriet Carr?

The thought was oddly disquieting, although Elizabeth refused to wonder why it should make a difference if

James gave up this job out of love for Harriet or simply because he'd grown tired of country living. She searched for a way to explain her fears and heard him sigh wearily.

'I can see you're still not convinced, Elizabeth. All I can do is hope that you'll try to keep an open mind. Now, I think we'd better get back, don't you?'

There seemed little to say after that. They drove back to Yewdale in a silence broken only by James's brief farewell when she dropped him off at the pub. Elizabeth drove the rest of the way home and parked in the drive. She got out of the car and made her way round the house to the back garden. Walking to the low fence, she took a deep breath and let the stillness of the night settle around her.

She often came to this spot when she got back from a call late at night. There was a special magic about this view of the towering majesty of the mountains, rising above the sleeping town. Usually a few minutes spent looking at it soothed away the strains and stresses of the day, but tonight it had little effect. Her mind seemed to be in turmoil, frothing with thoughts that made her feel tense and on edge...

She sighed as she made her way back to the house. It was going to take more than a wonderful view to cure what ailed her tonight. James Sinclair might have been in the town less than a day but already he was making his presence felt. And she had the nasty suspicion that this was only the beginning!

CHAPTER FIVE

'I THINK it sounds like an excellent idea. What does Liz have to say about it?'

David's voice carried through the open door and Elizabeth paused. It was Saturday morning and she wasn't due in surgery that day. They operated a system whereby only urgent cases were seen on Saturdays, taking turns to provide cover.

Elizabeth had been on her way to the hairdresser's when she'd realised that she'd left her wallet in her desk. Now she found herself hesitating as she wondered what was going on.

'I did mention it to her but I may as well be honest and admit that she had reservations.' There was amusement in James's voice, which immediately had Elizabeth's hackles rising. 'I get the impression that Elizabeth can be, well—a little set in her ways at times, shall we say?'

'Don't let Liz hear you say that!' David laughed affectionately, mercifully drowning out her horrified gasp.

How dared James pass such a judgement! she thought angrily. He'd been here less than a week so what right did he have to form opinions like that?

She realised that David was still speaking and moved to the door. Maybe she shouldn't be eavesdropping but it was hard to resist the temptation after that last outrageous statement. Exactly what was James up to?

'It could solve a lot of problems, though. Non-attendance rates for outpatient appointments could be cut for a start. A lot of people around here are loath to travel thirty miles to the hospital to see a consultant for five or ten minutes, but with this video link they'd only need to come into the surgery.'

'There are other advantages as well,' James put in. 'One of the biggest problems in rural practices is keeping in touch with other doctors. The video link could be used for that purpose too.'

'Sounds a great idea to me. Obviously cost is a big consideration but we might be able to get around that, as you suggested. I'm sure Liz will agree once she sees how much benefit everyone could derive from it.'

Elizabeth headed out of the door, not waiting to hear anything more. Maybe it was irrational, but she felt deeply hurt that James had gone behind her back like that...

'Hello! What are you doing here? I thought it was your morning off. Or did I get it wrong?'

She swung back at the sound of James's voice, unable to keep the hurt from her eyes as she looked at him. Since that night when they'd attended the accident together she'd tried her hardest to overcome her doubts about him. Even when she'd found herself thinking about what he'd told her about his relationship with Harriet Carr—and wondering if it really was over, as he'd claimed—she'd tried not to let it influence her feelings in any way.

Both David and Sam had been unstinting in their praise for the way James had settled in so quickly and, from the comments she'd heard, Elizabeth knew that the patients had accepted him readily enough. She'd tried to be fair and take all that into account but how fair was it of James to go to David and try to persuade him to take sides against her?

'Elizabeth?' he prompted, when she didn't answer.

'I forgot my wallet.' Elizabeth treated him to a chilly

smile. 'That's why I came in. How about you? What are you doing here this morning, James?' She gave a contemptuous laugh. 'Did you decide that it would be the perfect opportunity to talk David round to your way of thinking while I was out of the way, by any chance?'

'From that, I take it you overheard the conversation just now?'

The amusement in his voice did little to soothe her feelings. Elizabeth's eyes blazed with contempt as she faced him squarely. 'Yes, I heard. It hasn't taken you long to start causing ripples around here, has it? You've been here less than a week and already you're plotting behind my back.'

'Don't be ridiculous!' He grasped her arm, steering her swiftly into his room and closing the door before she could protest. His mouth was set into a tight line as he stared at her with cool blue eyes. 'There's no question of me going behind your back, Elizabeth. I outlined my suggestions to you the first day I got here.'

'And I told you my views on the subject. So what do you do? Go to David and try to win his support!' Elizabeth retorted. How dared he do that? And how dared he…he laugh at her! Irrational or not, that was probably the worst thing of all—the fact that he'd seen fit to make fun of her.

She felt sudden tears prick her eyes and turned away before he could see them, staring fixedly out of the window. 'I told you how I felt and that should have been enough.'

'I hate to remind you, but there are *three* partners in this practice, Elizabeth—three *equal* partners at that. None of us has the right of veto. If it comes to a decision then it must be made by majority vote.'

His tone was level almost to a fault. Elizabeth strove to match his composure, despite feeling so hurt. This had nothing to do with her personal feelings, she assured herself. In her *professional* opinion the video link would be of limited benefit, and that was all that mattered.

'Majority vote? This isn't a commercial enterprise. We aren't deciding how many shares to sell or what dividends to pay. This is the welfare of over seven thousand people we're talking about. But, if that's the way you prefer to see it, in my view the cost of setting up such a scheme would outweigh any possible advantages.'

'On the surface it may appear that way. However, if you take into account the number of man-hours it could save us you'll soon see that it would pay for itself very quickly.'

'Perhaps, although I'm not convinced about that. However, the money we spent on this project would have to come from somewhere.' She shrugged. 'What do you suggest, James? Should we shelve our plans for setting up a family planning clinic or forget about trying to increase the frequency of the baby clinic? Which of those do you think this community could do without, in your opinion? Because that's what this could all boil down to—the fact that we'd need to cut back on other services to set this up.'

'I've already explained that I would hope to get sponsorship for this, Elizabeth. And I am not suggesting that it should be set up at the expense of any other projects you have planned.' James shrugged. 'You know far more about the needs of this community than I do as yet.'

'Exactly!' she replied triumphantly. 'You've hit the nail on the head, James. You have no idea what this community does or doesn't want.'

'Maybe not. However, I do have the advantage of being able to take an objective look at how things are done around here. And I can see for starters that this practice is under tremendous pressure. Anything which alleviates that can only benefit everyone concerned—the patients *and* us.'

'That's your opinion. And, as far as I'm concerned, it counts for very little.' Elizabeth strode to the door and let herself out of the room, knowing that she couldn't bear to remain there a moment longer. It would be a waste of time, anyway, because it was obvious that she and James would never agree about this. Maybe he could be dispassionate about the way they ran this practice but she couldn't!

Leaving her car where it was, she walked into town. Yewdale House was set at the far end of the town, a little apart from the rest of the houses. Usually Elizabeth enjoyed the walk, especially on a day such as this.

It was a beautiful morning, the rain which had plagued them earlier in the week having given way to sunshine. The surrounding countryside was a riot of fresh spring greens, the expanse of blue sky broken only by a few wispy clouds, hovering over the mountains. However, she could draw little pleasure from it as she made her way along the high street. All she could think of was what James had done, how he'd deliberately gone behind her back and…and made fun of her!

'Morning, Dr Allen.'

She glanced around and summoned a smile as she saw Frank Shepherd, crossing the road. 'Morning, Frank. Lovely day.'

'It is. I'm off up to me dad's to help get the rest of the ewes in.' Frank sighed heavily. 'I did try having a word with him about being sensible, like, but it was like talking to the proverbial brick wall.'

'I know it isn't easy, Frank. Isn't there anyone you can get to help him with the farm?' Elizabeth suggested.

'I've been racking my brain but I can't think of no-

body. That's the trouble. I feel as though I should be
doing more but, to be honest, my time is limited to
weekends, what with my job and everything. Finding
somebody interested in working on the farm isn't easy,
believe me.' Frank sighed as he glanced along the
crowded street, as though he might find the answer to
the problem there.

Saturday mornings were always busy and today was
no exception. There were a few early tourists about, too,
Elizabeth noticed, obviously taking advantage of the
weather. Yewdale was so picturesque, with its quaintly
old-fashioned shops and tiny grey stone cottages, that it
attracted a lot of visitors, although most came later in
the year.

July and August were always hectic, the pavements
crowded with tourists. They brought a lot of money into
the town so they were made to feel welcome as many
local businesses relied on this valuable source of income
to keep them going through the winter months.

There was also an Outward Bound adventure school
on the banks of Yewdale Water, just two miles east of
the town, which brought in extra business. It catered
mainly for parties of children brought there on school
trips. Elizabeth could see a number of teenagers wandering along the street that day, laughing and joking as
they jostled each other.

All in all, it was a typical Saturday morning. It was
only she who felt different, uptight and angry after that
confrontation with James, but somehow she had to get
things into proportion and not allow it to upset her.

'How about asking Harvey Walsh over at Yewthwaite
Farm if he's got anyone he can spare to give your father
a hand during lambing?' she suggested, confining her
thoughts to the problem of Isaac Shepherd.

'I tried that. I saw Harvey in the Fleece last night but

he wasn't able to help. He's struggling himself as he's lost two of his men in the past month because they've moved away for better wages. He's only got one man left working for him now and his flock's three times the size of me dad's.'

'Then I don't know what the answer is, Frank. Somehow we're going to have to find Isaac some help otherwise that farm is going to kill him. I'll keep my ears open in case I hear of anyone.'

They parted company after that and Elizabeth carried on into town. She glanced at her watch and realised that she was rather early for her appointment at the hairdresser's. She headed for the café and sat at a table by the window. Maybe a cup of coffee would help to restore her to a better mood. Why on earth had she allowed herself to get so upset? It wasn't like her to react that way. But, then, she'd been acting strangely for the past week—

'Do you mind if I sit down?'

She glanced up as she recognised the deep voice, her heart leaping as she saw James standing by the table. It was on the tip of her tongue to refuse the request but he forestalled her.

'I'm unarmed, Elizabeth.' He held up his hands in a gesture of surrender, his blue eyes full of wry amusement. 'So don't shoot me down, will you?'

It was such a ridiculous thing to say that she found herself laughing, and James obviously took that to mean that he could join her. He shrugged off his jacket and draped it over the back of a chair, then sat down with a grimace.

'Look, let me say my party piece first, will you? I'm really and truly sorry if you thought I was trying to be devious. The last thing I want is for us to fall out over this.'

There was no mistaking the sincerity in his voice, but Elizabeth knew that it wasn't just the way he'd approached David that had hurt her. However, to admit that it was how he'd laughed at her was something she couldn't bring herself to do. It was a relief when the waitress arrived to take their order, sparing her from having to answer.

James sat back in his chair after the waitress had gone again. 'Busy little place, this. I have to confess that I never imagined the town would do such a brisk trade.'

'Saturday always tend to be a bit hectic. There aren't any supermarkets around here so most people shop in the high street,' she explained, glad to steer the conversation away from what had happened earlier.

'So I can see.' James turned to glance out of the window, watching the crowd passing along the street. He turned back to her and grinned. 'I think it's great to see people out and about like this. There's such a wonderful community feel to the place, isn't there, everyone knowing everyone else?'

'You don't find it a bit…well, overpowering?' Elizabeth waited while the waitress set the coffee-pot on the table along with the cups and saucers. Automatically, she reached for the pot and poured the coffee, handing a cup to James.

'Thanks. No, not so far. I'm still at the stage when everything is new and wonderful.' He stirred sugar into his coffee and put the spoon in the saucer with a sharp click, which brought her eyes to his face. 'Why *are* you so convinced that the novelty will wear off, Elizabeth? It's obvious that you love this town so why can't you accept that I'll grow to love it too? Is it so hard to believe that?'

Elizabeth looked away, not sure how best to answer the question. 'I don't know…' She took a quick breath, struggling to put her feelings into words. 'I suppose I have difficulty in accepting that this is really the kind of life for you, James.' She glanced up but his face gave little away so she struggled on. 'I mean, you're used to living in a city, and not just any city—London. Aren't you going to miss so many things, by being here?'

'Such as?' He picked up his cup, regarding her over the rim as he drank. His gaze was very steady, his blue eyes fixed intently on her. Elizabeth had the strangest feeling that what she said was important to him and that made it all the more difficult. Why should her opinion matter to him? she wondered. It didn't make any sense, just made her feel more confused than ever.

'Well, the theatre, the opera, the shops...a hundred and one things, I imagine, which you won't have access to around here.' She paused but there was no way she could avoid mentioning it when it had been at the forefront of her mind all week.

'And there's Harriet, of course. Surely you'll miss her? You were together for some time, you told me. What if you decide that you made a mistake and that...that you want to give your relationship another chance? That could alter things completely.'

'It could. But it won't happen. Harriet and I are—' He broke off as someone came rushing into the café and hurried over to their table.

'There you are, Dr Allen! I thought I'd spotted you, coming in here.'

Elizabeth forced a smile as she looked up. 'Hello, Mrs Rimmer. Is something wrong?'

'Yes, look.' Marion Rimmer pointed out of the window. Elizabeth saw that a small crowd was starting to gather outside the hairdressing salon across the street. 'It's one of them youngsters from the adventure centre— seems to be having some sort of a turn, he is. I saw what was happening so I came over to get you. I just happened to notice you, coming in here, while I was cleaning my windows,' Marion explained, shooting a coy glance at James. 'I didn't know that you were meeting someone, though, Dr Allen.'

Elizabeth sighed as she stood up. Marion Rimmer was the town busybody and spent a good deal of her time cleaning her windows. 'Dr Sinclair and I bumped into one another by accident, Mrs Rimmer.' She glanced at James, frowning as she saw the glimmer of amusement in his eyes. What was so funny?

'Oh, so you're the new doctor, are you? I heard you'd started. I hope you're settling in all right, Dr Sinclair.'

'I am. Thank you, Mrs. Rimmer.' James rose to his feet, smiling at the elderly widow before turning to Elizabeth with a lift of his brows. 'Shall we go and see if we're needed?'

Leaving Marion Rimmer staring after them, they left the café and hurried across the road. James pushed his way through the crowd of onlookers and knelt beside the young boy who was lying on the pavement.

'Did anyone see what happened?' he demanded, as he unzipped the teenager's jacket and unbuttoned the neck of his shirt. The boy was unconscious, his body rigid as he lay on the ground. When Elizabeth joined him she noticed that the lad's lips were faintly blue while his face and neck were congested with colour.

'Yes, I did. Well, we all did.' A young girl crouched beside her. 'Nick said he could smell something funny, and we were just making jokes about it being his socks when he suddenly gave this weird cry and fell down.'

'I see.' Elizabeth nodded, already fairly sure what was wrong with him. Her suspicions were immediately confirmed when the boy suddenly began to twitch violently. Slipping off her jacket, she cushioned his head with it as he began to thrash about on the pavement. His jaw was tightly clenched so that his breathing was noisy and laboured, but she knew that should last only for a few minutes and would present little danger.

'What's happening to him?' The girl was near to tears now, and the rest of the group looked on in horror at what was happening to their friend. Elizabeth sought to reassure them.

'Nick's having an epileptic seizure. He'll be perfectly fine in a few minutes... Look, it's starting to ease off already.'

The boy's muscles were beginning to relax and gradually his breathing became steadier. He was still unconscious but it wouldn't be long before he came round, Elizabeth guessed.

'An epileptic seizure? You mean a fit? But he never said... None of us knew... Did we?' The girl turned an imploring look on the rest of the party, who all shook their heads.

Elizabeth bit back a sigh. If Nick had been hoping to keep his epilepsy a secret, his plans had been well and truly thwarted. She glanced at James who grimaced, obviously of the same opinion.

'Let's get him on his side, shall we, Elizabeth?' he said. Between them they rolled Nick over and made him comfortable. After a few minutes his eyes slowly opened and he looked around dazedly.

'What happened? Where am I...?'

'You're OK. I'm a doctor so just take it easy.' James laid a restraining hand on the boy's arm as he tried to sit up. 'You're going to be fine as long as you give yourself a chance to come round properly.'

'Come round? I remember feeling odd...' Tears started to the boy's eyes before he quickly dashed them away with the back of his hand. 'I had a fit, right?'

'Seems like it. I take it you've had them before, then?' James's tone was matter-of-fact and seemed to steady the boy.

'Yes.' Nick looked up at the crowd, then turned beseechingly to Elizabeth. 'I want to get out of here!'

'Just as soon as you're fit enough to walk,' Elizabeth promised before she rose. 'Right, everyone, that's it. Nick's going to be fine. Thanks for all your help, but Dr Sinclair and I will see he gets home safely.'

She turned to the group of teenagers as the crowd began to disperse. 'I take it you're from the Outward Bound centre? Are any of the leaders with you?'

The girl shook her head. 'No, we walked into town by ourselves.' She glanced at Nick, who steadfastly avoided her gaze. 'Is...is Nick going to be all right now?'

'He'll be fine once he's had a rest. However, I don't think it would be a good idea for him to try walking back to the centre just yet. I'll drive him back in a few minutes,' James offered. 'I've room for two more if anyone wants to come along for the ride.'

'No!' Nick spoke up before any of his friends could answer. 'I mean, there's no point in spoiling everyone's day. I'd rather go back on my own.'

Elizabeth sensed that the girl wanted to object, but in the end she left with the others, casting worried glances over her shoulder as the party carried on down the high street.

'I'll just fetch my car,' James said quietly, as he drew Elizabeth to one side. 'Try and find out if he's on any medication, will you? I want to make certain that the people in charge of the centre know exactly what he's taking and what to do if this happens again.'

'They're usually very good there. Ian Farnsworth, the manager, is very reliable so there shouldn't be a problem about them keeping on eye on Nick. I'll find out what he's on, though,' she agreed.

'Good.' James gave her a warm smile before he hurried away. Elizabeth took a small breath, wondering why she felt a trifle breathless all of a sudden.

Deliberately, she blanked out the thought of why James's smile should have any effect on her as she went back to the boy. Jeannie Shepherd, Frank's wife, came out of the salon with a chair just then, and between them they helped Nick onto it.

'Why did it have to happen now?' Nick asked hoarsely, when Jeannie had hurried back to her clients. He ran a hand over his eyes, trying not to let Elizabeth see that he was crying. He couldn't have been more than seventeen and she could imagine how embarrassed he was because his friends had witnessed what had happened to him.

'Are you on any medication?' she asked, knowing that it was better to be pragmatic about it.

'Phenobarbitone,' he replied, studiously avoiding her eyes.

'And have you been taking it regularly, as prescribed?' She sighed when he shook his head. 'Nick, that's just being silly! You must know that you need to take the medication on a regular basis for it to be effective.'

'I didn't want people asking me what it was for!' His tone was suddenly fierce. 'You saw the way they were all looking at me just now, as though I'm some sort of...of freak!'

'People are often afraid when they see someone having an epileptic fit—that's why they react that way. They don't understand that it's just a sudden discharge of electricity inside the brain that causes it to happen, rather like lots of radio signals getting jumbled. If you ex-

plained that to your friends they'd be able to accept it
more readily if it ever happens again.'

'Think so? Take it from me that they won't! People
treat you differently after you've had a fit, as though
you're going to start acting like a weirdo or something,'
Nick replied hotly.

'Then that's an even better reason for making sure that
you take your medication on a regular basis. Doing that
will help minimise the number of attacks you have,
Nick.'

Elizabeth didn't add anything more because James arrived at that moment. She went over to the car, wanting
a word with him out of hearing of the boy. 'He's on
phenobarbitone but it seems that he hasn't been taking
it. And, from what I can gather, he hasn't told anyone
that he's epileptic either so you'd better have a word
with the staff at the centre.'

'I suspected as much. I'll have a word with this Ian
Farnsworth and bring him up to date on what's gone on,
although surely Nick's school will have alerted them? It
must be on his record.' James sighed as he glanced at
the unhappy teenager. 'Poor kid. It's stressful enough,
being his age, without this, but I'll impress on him that
he must start acting sensible from here on in.'

Between them they got Nick into the car. He was still
a bit shaky but Elizabeth knew he'd be fine after he'd
had a sleep. James slammed the door and picked up the
chair to carry it back to the salon, ignoring Elizabeth's
protest that she'd do it. He put it down inside the shop
then turned to her. His eyes were serious suddenly as
they met hers.

'I hope we've managed to straighten things out between us, Elizabeth. I don't want to be at cross purposes
with you.'

Elizabeth looked away, shaken by the intensity of his

gaze. 'I imagine it takes time to form a working relationship, James. Perhaps I'm a bit on edge with all the changes that have taken place recently around here.'

'It takes time to build *any* relationship, Elizabeth.'

He gave her a slow smile and left the salon. Elizabeth could feel her pulse, tapping away like crazy. What had James meant by that? she wondered dizzily.

She sighed as Jeannie called her over to the washbasins. What did it matter, anyway? Despite what he'd said, she was still convinced that he'd be on his way back to London in a few months' time, sick and tired of the demands of the job *and* eager to fall into the welcoming arms of the undoubtedly beautiful Harriet!

That it would prove she'd been right all along to have doubts about him gave her very little pleasure. It seemed she couldn't win.

CHAPTER SIX

ELIZABETH was in the sitting-room when the bell rang that evening. She heard Mrs Lewis go to answer it and frowned as she wondered who it could be. Getting up from the chair, she lowered the volume on the stereo just as the door opened and Sam O'Neill appeared.

'I hope I'm not disturbing you, Liz, but I thought I'd call round and see if you felt like coming to the Fleece. Abbie and David are going to be there—and James, of course. There's a darts match on between our local team and the one from the Lion over at the Newthwaite so I thought we should offer our support!'

Elizabeth forced a smile, trying not to let Sam see how little the idea appealed to her. She wasn't averse to spending an evening at the local pub, but the fact that James would be there set her frantically thinking up an excuse. Maybe it was silly but she didn't want to have to spend time with him that night as it might only serve to make her feel more mixed up than ever.

'Sounds great but I'm on call tonight,' she hedged. 'I think I'd better give it a miss.'

'Why? You can take your mobile and have any calls transferred to that.' Sam grimaced. 'Actually, there's a bit of an ulterior motive. Abbie's rather down today. Evidently, it would have been her daughter's birthday tomorrow. I thought this might help take her mind off it for a couple of hours.'

'I'd forgotten.' Elizabeth sighed. 'It must be hard for her. Losing the baby isn't something she'll find it easy to get over. She's always so bubbly that you tend to forget she's been through such a rough time, what with Megan dying and her marriage breaking up.'

'That's why I thought it would be good to get together and cheer her up.' Sam shrugged. 'Not that she's mentioned it, of course, but I could tell she was thinking about it when I saw her earlier today.'

Elizabeth smiled, wondering fleetingly if there was more to the easygoing friendship between Abbie and Sam than she'd realised. 'Then it's up to us to take her mind off it as best we can. All right, I'll come. Just give me a few minutes to arrange to have any calls transferred and I'll walk down with you.'

It took about ten minutes to walk to the Fleece, and on the way Sam told her all about the overseas job he'd be starting in the autumn. He was full of enthusiasm and Elizabeth sent up a silent prayer that there wasn't more to his relationship with Abbie than first appeared. Abbie had had enough heartache in the past few years. Surely she understood that Sam wasn't looking for commitment and was set on going overseas to work?

Elizabeth was still brooding about it as she pushed open the door to the pub. There was quite a crowd there that night to support the local darts team so it took her a moment to spot David and Abbie at a table in the corner. Elizabeth made her way over to join them, exchanging greetings with people on the way. Living and working in such a close-knit community meant that everyone knew who she was, but it was the part of the job she enjoyed most.

She found her thoughts turning back to what James had said that morning—about it being something he enjoyed about working in the town—but, then, it was early days yet and he had plenty of time to change his mind about that, as well as everything else!

'Hello, Elizabeth. Sam said that he was going to try to persuade you to come.'

As though she'd conjured him up by thinking about him, James suddenly appeared at her side. Elizabeth gave him a cool smile, annoyed that he made it sound as though for her to turn up at the pub was an occasion to be marked in red on the calendar! Was that how he saw her—as some stick-in-the-mud character who didn't enjoy a night out? In the light of the comment he'd made to David about her being set in her ways it seemed more than likely. The idea stung.

'You can see he succeeded, then, can't you?' She started to move on, but was stopped as James caught her arm.

'What have I said now? I seem to have a positive talent for putting my foot in it around you!' His voice grated with sudden impatience as he bent towards her.

Elizabeth swallowed, trying to dislodge the knot in her throat. This close to him she could see the tiny lines that fanned from the corners of his eyes and smell the clean scent of his skin. She felt her heart skip a beat as her senses responded immediately.

'Nothing. You're imagining it,' she said shortly, and deftly removed her arm from his grasp to wave to Abbie, who was watching them with a faintly quizzical expression on her face.

'Am I?' He smiled tightly as he glanced towards the table in the corner. 'Well, I suppose I'll have to take your word for that. So, what will you have to drink? It's my round.'

It was a relief to turn the conversation to such prosaic matters. Elizabeth knew she wouldn't have been able to come up with a reasonable explanation for the way she was behaving if he'd pressed her. 'Orange juice with ice, please. I'm on call tonight,' she answered quickly.

'Right. Abbie's saved you a seat. I'll bring the drinks over.'

Elizabeth took a deep breath as she headed across the room. Usually she had no difficulty in maintaining her composure, but she seemed to have such difficulty doing so around James!

'Hmm, now, what was that all about?' Abbie slid along the bench to make room for Elizabeth to sit next to her.

'All what?' Elizabeth asked as she squeezed into the gap.

'That very intense conversation you and the gorgeous Dr Sinclair were having just now.' Abbie rolled her eyes expressively. 'Could it be the start of something big, I wonder?'

'Certainly not!' Elizabeth retorted, then coloured as she saw Abbie's brows rise at the rather too heated denial.

'Methinks the lady doth protest too much, to quote a well-worn phrase.' Abbie lowered her voice so that it wouldn't carry to David and Sam, who were deep in discussion about which team would win the match that night. 'It isn't like you to lose your cool, Liz. Obviously something's rattled you or, rather, *someone*!' She glanced towards the bar and sighed theatrically. 'I can't blame you. James is rather dishy, isn't he?'

Elizabeth followed her gaze, her eyes immediately alighting on James's broad back as though some sort of inbuilt radar helped her pick him out. He was wearing jeans and a thin black polo shirt that night, and she found herself thinking how well they suited his leanly muscular physique. The outfit was no different to what most of the other men were wearing yet he seemed to stand out from the crowd gathered around the bar.

Was it because he was a newcomer to the town? she

wondered, then quickly dismissed the idea. James had a presence which would make him stand out no matter where he was.

Elizabeth felt her heartbeat quicken at the thought. It made her feel strangely guilty that she should have thought it. She started to look away, then realised that James was watching her in the mirror behind the bar. For a second her gaze meshed with his before she lowered her eyes, hating the fact that he'd caught her staring at him like some...some lovelorn teenager!

The comparison was so ridiculous that she felt embarrassed heat touch her cheeks, and hastily looked for a way to change the subject before Abbie put her own interpretation on its cause! 'Sam was telling me all about this new job of his on the way here,' she began, then wondered if that had been the best subject to introduce. However, Abbie didn't appear in the least bit concerned.

'I know. He's almost driven me mad this past week, going on and on about it! He keeps telling me to apply but it isn't my scene. I'm a homebody, I'm afraid. I like living here. I can't see myself wanting to leave—in the foreseeable future, at least.' She glanced up and grinned wickedly. 'Drinks at last! Thanks, James. There should be room for you to squeeze in next to Elizabeth...'

'Just!' James laughed as he handed round the glasses and squeezed into the gap. 'Sorry,' he murmured, as his thigh brushed Elizabeth's.

She gave him a quick smile, trying to ignore the flicker of awareness that flowed through her as he settled himself in the narrow space—but it was impossible. Each time he reached for his glass his arm brushed her shoulder or his thigh touched hers...

'I like your hair, by the way. Obviously, that little fracas this morning didn't have any disastrous consequences!'

'Thankfully not.' Elizabeth replied coolly enough, trying to quell the rush of pleasure she felt at the compliment. She took a sip of her orange juice, then quickly put down the glass when she found her hand was shaking. 'How…how did you get on at the centre?' she asked, to cover her nervousness, although what she had to be nervous about she had no idea. 'Did you speak to Ian Farnsworth?'

'Yes. Nice chap. It seems that no one there had any idea young Nick was epileptic. Usually that sort of information is passed on to them via the school, but it turns out that Nick only transferred to his present school a few months ago. Evidently, the head did send out a standard letter to his parents, asking for medical details, but Nick waylaid it.'

'Oh! Not that I'm surprised because it was obvious how embarrassed he was about it.' Elizabeth felt a rush of sympathy for the boy, even though he'd been foolish to pull such a stunt. 'How was he when you left?'

'Fine. I think I managed to impress on him how vital it is that he takes his medication as per instructions. And Ian promised that they'd keep a close eye on him. In fact, we had quite a chat. It seems that Ian is keen to improve their first-aid clinic so I offered to go over there and make a few suggestions, maybe give the staff a bit of extra training.' James shrugged. 'First-aid training is something I'm particularly interested in. It's invaluable, to my way of thinking.'

'Sounds like a good idea,' David put in, 'although it could be time-consuming.'

'I offered to do it in my own time so it shouldn't cause any problems at the surgery,' James explained quickly.

'So long as you don't go taking on too much,' David warned. 'We're stretched now so there's no point in you giving up all your free time as well. Still, maybe we can reorganise some of our routines and save time that way.'

Elizabeth picked up her glass, refusing to be drawn on that point. There was little doubt in her mind that David was alluding to the plan to introduce more technology into the daily work of the practice, but she still wasn't convinced it was a good idea.

Conversation moved along more general lines after that. The opposing darts team arrived, and after drinks had been consumed the match started. Sam O'Neill got roped in to play when one of the Fleece's regular players failed to turn up. He put up a pretty good show but the home team was still beaten.

There was a lot of good-natured grumbling over more pints of the local brew. Harry's wife, Rose, had laid on a buffet supper and she invited everyone to join in. Elizabeth had barely had time for a mouthful of the delicious ham sandwiches, however, when her phone rang. It was Annie Jackson to say that Chloe was running a temperature again.

Elizabeth assured her that she would be there right away and rose to her feet. She was surprised when James got up as well. 'You don't need to come. You're not on duty tonight so stay and enjoy yourself.'

'I'd like to come, if you don't mind. I know the blood tests aren't back yet but I still can't help thinking that this is something more than just an infection.' He glanced at the others with mock severity. 'Save me some supper, you lot!'

'You'll be lucky!' Sam grinned as he helped himself to another sandwich. 'Still, you can always try appealing to Liz's soft heart. Maybe she'll fix you something.'

'Hmm, maybe.' James sounded so sceptical that Elizabeth flushed. She caught the look David shot her and turned away. She didn't want to have to explain that she and James didn't always see eye to eye—it would only worry him.

'Actually, I think I'll call it a night too.' David got up as well. 'Emily and Mike are staying with Kate's mother for the weekend so I'm going to take advantage of having the house all to myself for a change. There's a late night film on TV that I've been wanting to see for ages—that's if I don't fall asleep in the middle of it!'

Everyone laughed sympathetically. They'd all been under a great deal of pressure recently and knew how it felt to be so tired that they fell asleep at the drop of a hat. David walked to the door with them and waited while James ran upstairs to get his bag. He looked so tired that Elizabeth's heart went out to him.

'Maybe you should think about getting away for a break,' she suggested quietly.

'Oh, I don't know. I don't think it's fair to James to land him in at the deep end just yet.'

'He should have thought about what he was getting into before he signed the contract!' Elizabeth couldn't keep the sting out of her voice and she saw David's brows rise.

'That's a bit harsh, Liz. I'm sure James gave this partnership a great deal of thought before he decided to come in with us. You know as well as I do how long it takes to get the hang of a new job, not to mention a whole new area. Frankly, I'm more than happy with the way he's fitting in so well but obviously you still have reservations about him. Why? What has he done to make you feel this way?'

If only she knew! Elizabeth thought worriedly, but there was no way that she could confess how mixed up she felt.

'I...I suppose I'm having trouble adapting to the new situation,' she fudged.

'I know it must be hard, Liz. You must miss your father, but realistically you knew he'd retire some day.' David patted her hand. 'It'll work out, I promise you that. Just give James a chance and you'll see that having him on board will inject new life into the practice. Why, I was only saying to him this morning how I wished we could make better use of all this modern technology, and he came up with this brilliant idea—' David broke off and laughed.

'But he's already explained it to you, hasn't he? I hope you come round to the idea, Liz, because it seems like a step in the right direction to me.'

'I…I'll think about it, David,' she muttered, when he paused. *David* had introduced the subject? She'd assumed that James had done so—had deliberately sought out David to gain his support—but it seemed she'd been wrong…once again!

'Good for you!' David brushed her cheek with an affectionate kiss. 'And also think about what I said about giving James a chance, will you?'

He gave her a last encouraging smile before he headed out of the door. Elizabeth stayed where she was, her hand straying abstractedly to her cheek. The kiss had been no more than a token, although once she would have been thrilled even with that. Yet tonight it had left her feeling completely unmoved…

'You should listen to the doctor, Elizabeth.'

There was a teasing note in James's voice as he came down the stairs, and Elizabeth turned to him in confusion. 'I beg your pardon?'

'Remember that advice I gave you about David? Life's too short to waste so let him know how you feel!' He flicked her cheek with the tip of his finger, his eyes mocking her when she jumped. 'A woman needs more than the odd chaste kiss to look forward to.'

He opened the door for her, without adding anything else, but, then, he'd said quite enough! Elizabeth tried to whip up her anger but she couldn't seem to achieve the result she wanted. Her hands clenched as she stepped out into the street, and the urge to touch her cheek again was almost overwhelming. David's kiss might have made very little impression but her skin was definitely tingling now...from when James had touched it!

'When did Chloe's temperature start to rise again, Mrs Jackson?'

James coiled up his stethoscope and drew the sheet over the child's hot little body. Chloe's temperature was hovering around the 39.5°C mark, a definite cause for concern.

'About an hour ago. Oh, she was off colour all day, crying and complaining that her legs hurt.' Annie Jackson sighed. 'I tried doing what you said, Doctor, and sponged her down, like, but it didn't seem to work so I thought I'd better call you.'

'You did the right thing, Mrs. Jackson.' James stated encouragingly. 'Have you noticed anything else, by any chance, apart from her saying her legs were hurting?'

'Well...' Annie hesitated. She glanced uncertainly at her husband, Barry, who was standing in the doorway, then seemed to make up her mind. 'Barry didn't want me to say owt in case you started thinking we'd done it, but we haven't, Doctor!' Annie turned beseechingly to Elizabeth. 'You know I love my kids, Dr Allen. Oh, I know I can be a bit quick-tempered, like, but I'd never hit any of them!'

'Of course not, Annie,' Elizabeth replied. She glanced at James and shrugged, as much in the dark as he was about what Annie meant. She gave the young woman an encouraging smile. 'Just tell us what you've noticed. It could be something important.'

'Bruises.' Annie went to the bed, drew back the sheet and pointed to Chloe's legs. 'I don't know where they've come from because she hasn't been out of the house all week. I asked her if she'd fell over but she says as she didn't.'

Elizabeth frowned as she saw the mass of bruises on the child's thin legs. 'I see what you mean.' She smiled at Chloe. 'And you can't remember hurting yourself— maybe when you've been playing with your brothers?'

Chloe shook her head, clutching the doll she was holding even tighter. She gave James a shy smile as he sat on the side of the bed, turning the doll so he could see that she'd pinned the star badge to its gaudy red and yellow dress.

'So your dolly's been a good girl, has she? Just like you?' He laughed as Chloe nodded then he gently examined the discoloured patches on her legs, before turning to her parents again. 'Is there anything else at all that you've noticed? It might seem very insignificant to you but it could be a big help in determining what's wrong with Chloe.'

'Well...' Barry Jackson shifted uneasily. A small, wiry man with over-long black hair and a tendency to avoid direct eye contact, he was obviously uncomfortable about being questioned like this. Elizabeth suspected that Barry's frequent run-ins with the local police had something to do with it!

'Her gums have been bleeding. It's happened a few times now and it happened again tonight,' he explained at last.

'I see.' James sounded thoughtful as he got up. 'Obviously, everything you've told us tonight must be taken into consideration. The test results should be back in a day or so. They should give us a better idea of what's wrong with Chloe. In the meantime, I'll give you some paracetamol syrup, which will reduce the fever, and do keep sponging her down because it will help.'

Annie saw them to the door. 'She'll be all right, won't she, Doctor? It is just some sort of infection?'

'We'll know more once the results come through, Mrs Jackson.' James smiled but Elizabeth noticed that he carefully avoided giving Annie a direct answer.

They walked back in silence, after leaving the Jacksons' cluttered terraced house. Elizabeth suspected that James had an idea what might be wrong with Chloe and that he wasn't happy about it. She glanced his way, seeing the frown that drew his brows together.

'You think you know what's wrong with Chloe, don't you?' she asked quietly.

'Yes.' He sighed heavily. 'I hope I'm wrong but I don't think so, unfortunately. I had a case similar to this in my last post, a child around Chloe's age with similar symptoms. It turned out that he was suffering from acute lymphoblastic leukaemia.'

'I see.' Elizabeth rapidly ran through the list of Chloe's symptoms, comparing them to those of leukaemia. 'Yes, you're right. The fever and swelling of the lymph glands and spleen, the bruising and bleeding, even those bouts of chest infection she had earlier in the year—'

'And let's not forget that rash,' James cut in. 'I knew I'd seen something like it before but I didn't make the connection until tonight!'

'You can't blame yourself for that. The rash could have been the result of any number of things—it still might be,' Elizabeth added, but without any real conviction.

'Think so?' James laughed softly. 'No, you're as con-

vinced as I am that this isn't just some minor infection,
but thanks for trying to cheer me up anyway.'

Elizabeth looked away, not liking the way her heart
had leapt when James had smiled at her. They'd reached
the Fleece and she paused, wondering once again why
she responded the way she did to a touch or a smile
from him. Was it just that she was always on her guard
around him and that was what made her more aware of
him than she might have been otherwise? It made sense
in one way but it was hard to accept it as the explanation.

'Well, I'd better let you get off home. I hope you have
a quiet night.'

'Thanks. So do I.' She summoned a smile as she
turned to him, unaware of the uncertainty that clouded
her hazel eyes.

'What is it, Elizabeth? Something's worrying you,' he
said. 'Is it Chloe?'

'I...I was just hoping that you were wrong about her,'
she said quickly, snatching at the excuse. If she seemed
unusually aware of James, didn't he appear just as...as
sensitive to her? He seemed to be able to tell when
something was troubling her and yet she couldn't understand how he was able to read her so easily when
few others could.

The church clock began to strike and Elizabeth took
the opportunity to escape from a situation with which
she wasn't comfortable. 'Eleven o'clock already! I'd better be off. As for Chloe, I suppose we'll have confirmation soon enough if it is leukaemia. We'll just have
to wait and see.'

'I suppose so. Goodnight, Elizabeth.'

His voice carried after her as she hurried away. When
Elizabeth got home she found that Mrs Lewis had gone
to bed, although she'd left the hall light burning.
Elizabeth switched it off before she went upstairs and

got ready for bed. She slid between the crisp cotton sheets and closed her eyes but sleep proved elusive. Fragments of what had gone on that day kept flashing into her mind, keeping her awake as the church clock chimed another hour.

She should have followed David's example and stayed up to watch the late film, she thought ruefully. She could even have gone round to his house to join him. Maybe it *was* time to let him know how she felt...

She fell asleep on that thought, yet when she woke the next morning it was to the realisation that it hadn't been David who'd filled her dreams the night before.

Elizabeth tossed back the quilt. She caught a glimpse of herself in the mirror on the dressing-table and deliberately whipped up her anger, preferring that to any of the other emotions she was feeling.

Wasn't it bad enough that she had to work with the wretched man every day? What right did James Sinclair have to be in her dreams all night long as well!

CHAPTER SEVEN

'IF YOU could pop in to see Isaac Shepherd, I'd be grateful, Abbie. I know it's a bit out of your way but you're going over to Yewthwaite Farm and it's in the same direction.' Elizabeth put two cups of coffee on the desk.

'Thanks.' Abbie took a sip of coffee and sighed. 'I'll see what I can do, but Frank warned me that his father won't exactly welcome me with open arms.'

'That's an understatement!' Elizabeth laughed as she picked up her own cup. It was Monday morning and surgery wasn't due to start for half an hour yet. However, whenever possible, they tried to set aside this time to discuss any problems which might arise during the coming week. It was something her father had always done, although it had tended to go by the board in the past few months due to sheer pressure of work.

She glanced up as Sam O'Neill came into the room to join them, yawning widely.

'Morning.' He ambled over to the coffee-pot and poured himself a wake-up dose of caffeine, shuddering appreciatively as he took the first sip. 'Ah-h, that's better! Gets the old grey cells whizzing around.'

'It'll take more than a cup of coffee to wake them up from the look of you!' Abbie retorted. 'What were you up to last night?'

'Not what you're thinking! If I look half-dead it's because I was called out three times.' Sam sighed. 'I wouldn't have minded except that I met this girl on Saturday at the darts match and invited her round for supper. I'd no sooner got the microwave going than the first call came in. I told her I wouldn't be long but she said that if she'd wanted to sit in the house all by herself she could have stayed at home!'

'She had a lucky escape, if you ask me. Supper, indeed! That's a new name for it!' Abbie shot back pithily, before turning to Elizabeth again. 'Anyway, to get back to Isaac Shepherd, I'll try to catch him. Do you want me to check his blood pressure and so on—all the usual things?'

'Yes, and have a word with him about being sensible. Maybe you can get through to him—neither Frank nor I seem to be able to.'

Elizabeth glanced around again as David and James arrived together. She nodded to them, then continued to run through the list of patients Abbie was to see that day, yet all the time they were discussing potential problems Elizabeth was aware of James as he moved about the room and poured himself and David coffee.

She'd tried not to read too much into the way she'd dreamt about him the other night. After all, James had been the last person she'd spoken to, before going to bed on Saturday, so it was little wonder he'd popped up in her dreams, she'd reasoned. Suddenly the explanation seemed less plausible than it had done. How often did she dream about Mrs Lewis or her father, for instance—or even David, for that matter?

'Liz?'

She started as Abbie said her name, flushing as she saw the curious look the other woman gave her. 'Sorry, I was just wondering if there was anything we could do about Harvey Walsh's mother,' she invented hurriedly. 'It can't be easy for them to cope now the old lady's bedridden.'

'It isn't.' Abbie followed her lead but there was a note in her voice that warned Elizabeth that she'd seen through the lie. 'Helen Walsh has been run off her feet, trying to look after her as well as see to the hundred and one other jobs which need doing around the farm. That's why Helen had that fall down the stairs the other night. She was in such a rush that she didn't look where she was going, she told me.'

'It was a bad sprain, too,' David put in as he joined them, a cup of coffee in his hand. 'It will be a while before that ankle is completely better. She needs to rest it.'

'That's why I'm going there today—to give old Mrs Walsh a bath. Helen can't get up and down the stairs at the moment. But something needs to be done. They can't keep on like this much longer,' Abbie added worriedly.

'Is there no way that the old lady can have respite care to give the family a break?' James suggested. 'The situation is only going to get worse, from the sound of it.'

Elizabeth nodded. 'Yes, that makes sense. A couple of weeks to get back on her feet and Helen will be more able to cope, although I'm not certain how old Mrs Walsh will take to the idea. She's a bit of a martinet,' Elizabeth explained when James looked blank as they all laughed. 'Even at ninety and bedridden, Mrs Walsh still manages to rule that household!'

'She can't be that bad,' James protested, laughing.

'Wait until you meet her!' Elizabeth retorted. 'She'll soon have you dancing to her tune...like we all do!'

'I can't imagine her getting the better of you, Elizabeth,' James said softly, as the other three laughed again. 'I imagine it takes quite a lot to ruffle you.'

'That depends.' Elizabeth managed to smile but she couldn't deny the way her heart was beating a shade faster than normal. In other circumstances she might have agreed that it took a great deal to disconcert her, but the way she'd been acting recently had put paid to that claim!

She pushed the thought to the dimmest, darkest corner of her mind, not comfortable with the idea of who was responsible for her strange behaviour. Ever since James had arrived in Yewdale it seemed that she'd had trouble staying on an even keel. 'Anyway, Abbie, have a word with Helen and see what she says. So, any other problems?'

'No, I think that's it. See you later.' Abbie headed off on her rounds, leaving the others to finish their meeting.

'I've been thinking about that video link all weekend, and I really believe it could be of benefit to us.' David turned to Elizabeth. 'Have you given it any more thought, Liz?'

'Not really.' Elizabeth picked up her cup, wishing that David hadn't introduced the subject again. However, it appeared that he didn't intend to let it drop this time. When Sam asked what he was talking about David went into a lengthy explanation, which was met with some enthusiasm from the younger man.

'Sounds a great idea to me. Can't see what you're waiting for,' Sam enthused. 'Even if the hospital is a bit slow to give the go-ahead, a more sophisticated PC will still be worth its weight in gold. There are programmes geared to helping you diagnose a patient's problem, for instance. You feed all the information into the computer—symptoms, medical history, whatever—and the computer runs a check-list of possibilities.'

'A good GP doesn't need a computer to assist in diagnosing a patient's illness!' Elizabeth retorted, instantly disliking the idea.

'Why not? We use all sorts of diagnostic techniques nowadays—CT scanning, magnetic resonance imaging, positron emission tomography, to name just a few.'

James's tone was challenging. 'Patients' lives are being saved daily because of that kind of technology so how can you say that we shouldn't make use of everything available to us?'

'I'm not,' Elizabeth replied sharply. 'Obviously, all those are invaluable aids. I'm merely saying that an experienced practitioner doesn't require the latest gimmicks in his day-to-day work. What he needs is a genuine commitment to his patients. No computer in the world can replace that!'

Abbie suddenly reappeared to ask Sam to move his car as he was blocking her in. They had just disappeared, bickering about it being Sam's fault for parking too close or Abbie's for not being able to manoeuvre her car properly, when Eileen stuck her head round the door to inform them there was an urgent call.

'I'll take it,' David offered, hurrying from the room.

James waited until the door closed before he turned to Elizabeth again. His blue eyes were like ice as they rested on her. 'Nobody is saying that a computer can take the place of a doctor. It is simply a useful tool. However, I don't think that's really the issue here, is it, Elizabeth? The key word in what you just said was "commitment". And obviously you don't believe that's something I understand—in relation to this practice, at least!'

James left the room, without giving her time to answer. Elizabeth took a quick breath, shaken by the exchange. Was she allowing her doubts about James's suitability to influence her thinking on the subject? She didn't think so but it was obviously what he believed! The last thing she wanted was for there to be an atmosphere of friction between them when it would only affect the smooth running of the practice.

Elizabeth glanced at her watch and hurried from the

room when she saw there were still five minutes left before surgery began. Crossing the corridor, she knocked on James's door before she gave herself time for second thoughts. An apology was warranted, it seemed, and it had to come from her!

'Come in.' James glanced up as she entered the room. 'Yes?'

There was just enough chill in his voice to make her cheeks grow warm. Elizabeth was sorely tempted to walk out of the room again, but the thought of the disruption that could cause stopped her. She owed James an apology, it appeared, and that was exactly what he would get—even if it choked her!

'I came to say that I'm sorry. I didn't mean to imply that you aren't committed to the welfare of your patients,' she said tersely.

'Didn't you?' He gave a scathing laugh. 'I suppose I must give you the benefit of the doubt but I have to say I'm sceptical, Elizabeth. Ever since I arrived you've made no bones about the fact that you doubt my sincerity.'

It was nothing less than the truth but that didn't stop Elizabeth's temper from rising. The least he could have done was to accept her apology in the spirit in which it had been made!

'Now, now, Elizabeth, you're supposed to be pouring oil on troubled waters, not setting light to it!' James suddenly grinned as he leaned back in his chair and regarded her with amused eyes. 'It's odd, but people often remark on how calm you always are. They never make any mention of your temper, although I suppose it's only to be expected with that hair.'

'My hair?' Completely nonplussed by the remark, Elizabeth could only stare as James got up and came round the desk.

'Mmm, they always say that redheads have quick tempers, don't they?' He reached out, lifted a strand of hair from behind her ear and ran it gently through his fingers.

'It...it isn't red,' she muttered inanely. She took a quick breath, feeling her lungs burn as though all the air had been sucked out of them when she felt his knuckles brush her cheek. 'It's auburn.'

'At first glance maybe, but if you look closer you can see the fiery glints underneath.' His voice dropped, sounding deeper than ever, so that she felt a tremor run through her inch by disturbing inch. 'A little like you, Elizabeth. Cool enough on the outside to fool most people but the fire is there all the same.'

She didn't know what to say. It was only as she heard the door open that she moved so that her hair slid from James's grasp. She looked around, struggling to get a grip on herself, as David put his head around the door.

'I'm having to go out. That was Fred Murray on the phone. One of his men has had an accident with a tractor. Eileen's going to redirect my patients until I get back so I'm afraid you might find yourselves under siege for the next hour,' he informed them hurriedly. He started to leave but paused as he glanced warily from one to the other. 'Is everything all right?'

'Fine. Elizabeth and I don't quite see eye to eye about the value of this video link, but a truce has been declared,' James informed him dryly.

David laughed. 'Thank heavens for that! I'll see you later, then.'

He was gone in a trice, the door slamming behind him as he hurried off. James's face held a quizzical expression as he turned to Elizabeth.

'I hope I wasn't being too optimistic. Can you and I sort out our differences about this, do you think? I'm willing to give it a shot if you are.'

'Of course.' It seemed churlish to say anything else in view of the fact that she'd come specifically to apologise to him.

'Good. Let's shake on it, then.' James held out his hand and Elizabeth had no option but to take it. As she felt the warm strength of his fingers, closing around hers, she was beset by doubts once again. Was it possible that they could find common ground when their views seemed diametrically opposed?

She wanted to believe that they could, but as she went back to her room she knew in her heart that she still wasn't sure. It was going to take more than a handshake to convince her that James was the perfect partner for this practice!

The next few days were hectic. Elizabeth couldn't remember the practice ever being so busy. Both morning and evening surgeries were filled to capacity and she was called out twice on Wednesday night for good measure. By the time Thursday lunchtime arrived she was ready to drop. Fortunately it was her free afternoon, which meant that after she'd caught up with a mountain of paperwork she could take a little time for herself. She was just thinking longingly about a long hot soak in the bath when there was a tap on her door and James appeared.

'Have you got a minute, Elizabeth?'

'Of course.' She fixed a determined smile on her face as he came into the room. They'd had little chance to talk since Monday morning but that didn't mean she'd forgotten what had happened then. Far too many times she'd found her mind straying back to it...to their argument and her apology, to the way he'd fingered that strand of her hair...

'So, what's bothering you?' she asked quickly, push-

ing the memory to the back of her mind and hoping it
would stay there.

'The test results are back on Chloe Jackson.'

'And it's what you suspected?' Elizabeth asked softly,
knowing the answer even before he nodded.

'Yes. The blood tests show massive numbers of abnormal white cells present,' he replied simply.

'Oh, what a pity! So, what happens next? More tests?'

'Yes. They'll need to do a bone marrow biopsy then
probably a lumbar puncture to examine the cerebrospinal
fluid to check for blast cells.

'I'm on my way to the Jacksons' house to tell them.
Chloe will need to be admitted to hospital immediately
as the sooner they start the treatment the better her
chances are. I was wondering if you'd like to come with
me.' He shrugged. 'You know the family better than I
do and they might find it easier to hear the news from
you as I'm still a stranger to them.'

'Of course.' Elizabeth was surprised by his sensitivity.
She smiled at him, trying to ignore the way it made her
feel to be made aware yet again of how wrong she'd
been in her assessment of him. 'I've just got a few notes
to write up but it will only take me...oh, ten minutes at
most.'

'Fine. I'll meet you outside.' He looked back as he
turned to leave and his eyes seemed bluer than ever as
they rested on her. 'Thanks, Elizabeth. It's the sort of
job none of us likes doing, but it'll be easier if we do it
together, don't you think?'

He was gone before she could say anything. Elizabeth
cleared up, trying not to think too hard about the reason
for the warm glow lodged in her heart. It certainly felt
better to work in harmony with James than to be in con-
flict with him!

*   *   *

'Leukaemia!' Annie Jackson stared at them as though she couldn't quite take in what she was hearing. 'But I thought it was just a bit of a bug or something... Are you sure?'

'Yes, I'm afraid so.' James's tone was very gentle. 'The blood tests show massive numbers of abnormal white cells so there's no doubt at all.'

'White cells... I'm sorry, Dr Sinclair, but I don't understand any of this!' Annie turned to her husband. 'Do you, Barry?'

'No. I mean, I've heard about leukaemia but I've not taken much notice what it means, to tell the truth.' Barry ran a hand over his face. Elizabeth could see how shaken he was and felt a rush of sympathy for him and Annie. She chose her words with care, not wanting to upset them more than they already were.

'Chloe's body is producing abnormal white blood cells. Usually, the white cells fight infection, but in her case these abnormal cells are taking over and not allowing her to produce enough normal blood cells, either red ones or white. These abnormal cells have to be destroyed.'

'I see. And how will they do that?' Barry sounded a little less tense as he began to understand.

'Chloe will be given a series of blood transfusions in the hospital, as well as drugs which will kill off the white cells. However, the drugs can't distinguish between the abnormal cells and the proper ones so it means that Chloe will be very susceptible to any sort of infection, which is why they'll keep her in hospital during the treatment,' James explained carefully.

'And that will be it?' Annie asked hopefully. 'Once she's had these drugs and things she'll be cured?'

'It might take more than one course of treatment, Annie. We simply don't know at this stage. All I can

say is that Chloe has a good chance of making a full
recovery because her condition has been diagnosed so
quickly, thanks to Dr Sinclair.'

At that moment the door opened and Chloe appeared.
The child looked at them uncertainly then went straight
over to stand beside James's chair.

'Hello, Chloe,' he said softly. 'I've come to tell your
mummy and daddy that you'll be going into hospital
tomorrow so they can make you better. What do you
think about that?'

Chloe looked at him with big, solemn eyes. 'Will you
be there?'

'I'll come to visit you, certainly. And Dr Allen will,
I'm sure.' He glanced at Elizabeth for confirmation.

'Of course I shall. In fact, I bet you'll have lots of
people wanting to visit you,' Elizabeth said immediately.
She got up, as did James, knowing that the Jacksons
needed some time to take it all in.

Annie saw them to the door, her thin face white and
strained. 'She will be all right, Doctor?' she asked, looking to James for assurance. 'They will be able to cure
her?'

'I'm sure she'll be fine.' He patted her arm kindly.
'But it will take time, Mrs Jackson. You must be prepared for that.'

'I don't know how I'm going to manage, getting to
the hospital, what with the others to look after...'

'I tell you what—how about if I drive you and Chloe
there tomorrow? That way I can see her settled in and
have a word with the consultant in charge of her case,'
James offered.

'Oh, would you? I've never liked hospitals, you see.'
There was relief in Annie's voice as she accepted his
offer. James made arrangements about what time he'd

pick them up the following day, then led the way back to his car.

'That was good of you,' Elizabeth said as she got in beside him. 'Isn't it your free afternoon tomorrow?'

'Yes, but, then, it's yours today and you were willing enough to give it up, weren't you, Elizabeth?'

His tone was clipped, making her think that she'd offended him somehow. Elizabeth stared at him in confusion and suddenly gasped. 'That wasn't a dig at you, James! I wasn't implying that you shouldn't be giving up your free time because you're only the newcomer!'

'No?' he sounded unconvinced.

'No! It never crossed my mind. I meant what I said— it *is* good of you to give up your free afternoon.'

'I see.' He gave a rueful laugh as he slid the key into the ignition. 'I'm sorry, Elizabeth. I'm a bit touchy where Chloe is concerned.'

'Why? What do you mean?'

'Oh, just that I can't stop thinking that I should have realised what was wrong with her straight away.' His face was shadowed as he turned to her. 'There's no excuse because I'd seen the symptoms before—or some of them, at least.'

'But that's ridiculous!' Elizabeth laid her hand on his arm in an instinctive gesture of comfort. 'The symptoms Chloe was presenting could have been the result of any number of things! As it was, you arranged to have those tests done immediately, and you know as well as I do that they're the only true indication of leukaemia. Nobody could have done more for Chloe than you did, James.'

'Think so?' His expression softened as he looked at her in a way that made Elizabeth feel breathless all of a sudden. When he covered her hand with his she felt the jolt her pulse gave. 'Thank you, Elizabeth. It means a lot to hear you say that.'

He stared at her for a moment longer then started the engine. As they drove the short distance to the surgery she tried not to think too hard about the way he'd looked at her just now with such...such warmth!

James dropped her off then drove away to the do the rest of his calls. Elizabeth sighed as she watched the car disappear from view. No matter if they were arguing or agreeing—just being around James was unsettling, it seemed!

CHAPTER EIGHT

THE week finally came to an end and Sunday arrived. Elizabeth had been planning a lie-in but she woke just before seven. She got up and went downstairs to make herself some coffee, drinking it as she stood by the window.

It had been a busy week and all of them had worked flat out to keep up with the constant flood of patients, but she knew that it wasn't just tiredness which had left her feeling so drained. Working with James was having more of an effect than she'd realised. Was it just that she still wasn't convinced he was the right man for the job? Or was there another reason why she felt so on edge around him all the time?

It was still impossible to know the answer, and thinking about it made things worse rather than better! Elizabeth took a deep breath as she made up her mind to put the problem right out of her head, at least for that day. The next twenty-four hours were going to be a 'James-free' zone. Maybe that would help to put things back into perspective!

Determined to put her plan into action with immediate effect, she made herself some breakfast and sat at the table to read the Sunday papers. She was engrossed in the latest gossip when Mrs Lewis put her head round the kitchen door a short time later.

'I'll be off to church, then, Miss Elizabeth. I thought I'd go to the early service as I want to pop in to see my Ruth on the way back. She's driving over to Manchester to see my grandson, Robert, and I've baked a cake for

her to give him. But I won't be late back. I know you'll
be wanting your lunch.'

'Why don't you go with her?' Elizabeth put down the
paper and smiled at the housekeeper. 'I know how fond
you are of Robert, Mrs Lewis, and I'm sure he'd love
to see you.'

'Oh, I don't know about that…' Mrs Lewis hesitated,
obviously tempted by the idea. 'There's the lunch to see
to and I've no idea what time we'll get back.'

'Never mind about lunch. It doesn't seem worth going
to the trouble of cooking a big meal in the middle of the
day, with father not being here.' Elizabeth got up and
determinedly steered Mrs Lewis along the hall. 'Now, I
won't hear another word. Off you go and enjoy yourself.
Oh, and tell Robert that I want to hear all about university when he comes home for the holidays.'

'I will. Oh, it will be nice to see him again. I really
miss not having him around. If you're sure now…?'

'Quite sure. Now go along or you'll be late for
church!' Elizabeth laughed as Mrs Lewis hurried off,
spurred on by the thought. She closed the door and took
a deep breath. She'd wanted some time to herself and
now she intended to make the most of every single minute of these twenty-four hours!

Hurrying upstairs, Elizabeth quickly showered and
dressed in old jeans and a peach sweatshirt. She ran a
brush through her hair then pushed her feet into a pair
of comfortable trainers and ran back downstairs.

The air was sweet and clean as she stepped out of the
door, a hazy wash of lemon sunshine hinting at what
was to come. She headed away from the town, taking
the path which eventually led onto the slopes of the surrounding hills. The exercise would do her good and it
would definitely stop her brooding about things she
couldn't change!

A few early bees hummed in and out of the bushes that ran alongside the path. The sound was all that disturbed the peace of the day, and Elizabeth smiled in pleasure. This was her favourite time of the year, before all the tourists found their way to the area.

She followed the path for roughly a mile before she reached the fork. One way led past David's house and for a moment she debated whether to call in on him, before deciding against it. David had so little time with the children as it was that she hated to intrude.

She smiled wryly as she carried on, wondering what James would say about that, but she had no intention of forcing the issue, as he'd suggested. It wasn't her way of doing things. Was that what *he* preferred—for a woman to be open about her feelings? Was that how Harriet had been? From what James had said, Harriet had made no bones about how she'd felt about coming to live in Yewdale. Ultimately, it might be Harriet who was the biggest influence on whether or not he stayed...

Elizabeth felt a spurt of irritation as she realised where her thoughts had landed once again. She picked up her pace until her feet were flying along the path. Hadn't she just decided to keep the wretched man out of her mind for this one day? It was ridiculous that she couldn't manage even that...

'"Dr Livingstone, I presume?"'

Elizabeth came to an abrupt halt as she recognised the teasing voice, her heart racing crazily when she spotted James who was sitting astride a gate a few yards up ahead.

'Sorry, I didn't mean to startle you.' James gave her a rueful grin. 'Obviously you didn't see me, although it's no wonder. You seemed to be in rather a rush.'

'Er...no. I didn't,' Elizabeth muttered, recalling only too clearly the reason she'd been racing along like that.

'What are you doing here?' she asked quickly to cover her confusion. 'Are you out for a walk?'

'Yes and no.' He grinned as he saw her bewilderment at the ambiguous answer. He jumped down from the gate and came over to her, his eyes making a swift yet thorough assessment of what she was wearing so that Elizabeth was instantly conscious of the casual clothes she'd put on that day. However, there was nothing other than disconcerting appreciation in them as they arrived back at her face.

Elizabeth gulped in a little air to ease the restriction that seemed to have affected her breathing all of a sudden. 'Yes and no? What do you mean?'

'Well, I was intending just to go for a walk, but Harry mentioned something about there being a couple of houses up for sale. I decided to kill two birds with one stone, so to speak, and have a look at them while I was out.' He shrugged. 'The trouble is, I seem to be lost!'

'Lost?' Elizabeth couldn't help laughing. 'How on earth can you be lost? Yewdale isn't big enough to get lost in!'

'Maybe it's a piece of cake to you, Miss Clever Clogs, but to follow these paths isn't easy for a poor ex-city dweller, believe me!' James's smile took the sting out of his words. His face was full of amusement as he turned to look back along the footpath. 'I must have gone wrong somewhere, probably back where the path divides into two.'

'Probably,' she agreed, feeling a little easier as the conversation progressed. So what if she'd bumped into James? What difference did it make? Wasn't it the perfect opportunity to prove that she could treat him the same as anyone else?

Buoyed up by that thought, she gave him an encouraging smile. 'Where exactly are you trying to get to?

You said there were two houses you wanted to see, but I can't for the life of me think which they are.'

'Harry wrote them down for me, along with instructions on how to get there—not that they helped all that much.' James sighed. 'One path looks much the same as another to the uninitiated!'

Elizabeth laughed, amused by the way he was so ready to admit that he was confused. The James Sinclair she'd had summed up would have been very chary of admitting to any hint of weakness, but once again she'd been proved wrong...

'Let me have a look and see if I can point you in the right direction,' she offered quickly, as that disconcerting thought popped into her mind before she could stop it.

'Would you? I'd appreciate that, otherwise I could be wandering around here for the next week and still not find either of the places!' James handed her the piece of paper, pointing to the scrawled map. 'I know I came down here but after that...well!'

She studied the map, concentrating solely on making sense of it rather than allowing any other stray thoughts to pop into her head. She laughed out loud as she realised where it was leading to. 'The old Harper property is one of the places you want to view?'

'Yes. I'm sure that's the name Harry mentioned. Why?' James bent to look at the paper as though it might hold the key to what had amused her. Elizabeth felt her pulse leap as she caught the tangy aroma of the aftershave he'd used that morning. He was dressed as casually as she was that day, in jeans and a deep blue sweater, but that didn't stop her from suddenly being achingly conscious of the power of his lean, muscular body...

'Come on, Beth, tell me what's wrong with the place.'

There was warm amusement in his voice, which gave the diminutive added intimacy. Coming on top of how she was feeling already, it was little wonder she couldn't keep the tremor from her voice. 'You…you'll see for yourself. I…I'd hate to spoil the surprise.'

'Surprise?' James groaned. 'This is sounding worse by the second! Harry assured me that both these properties would be suitable for me. If he was pulling my leg…'

'I suppose it depends how desperate you are to find a place to live,' Elizabeth said quickly, willing herself to sound normal again. What *was* the matter with her? Why did she react like this around him? Once again the answers eluded her.

'Pretty desperate, I suppose. Harry's son is coming home in a few weeks time and evidently the room I'm renting at present belongs to him. I could do with finding a place, otherwise I could be out on the street.'

Elizabeth frowned as she focused her thoughts on what he'd said, although how long she could hope to keep them there was open to speculation! 'I'm sure it won't come to that. I'm surprised to hear that Adrian is coming home. He hasn't been back to Yewdale for some time now.'

'Is there some mystery about the boy?' James plucked a long blade of grass and nibbled at it with strong white teeth. 'Harry was very reluctant to go into detail about where his son has been, which isn't like him.'

'Adrian has been undergoing treatment in a psychiatric unit, but Harry and Rose don't speak about it so I'm not certain what the problem is exactly.' Elizabeth sighed as she ran a finger over one of the shiny green hawthorn leaves on the nearby hedge. 'You know how loath people are to talk about such things, especially when it affects a member of their own family.'

'Tough. Mental illness carries such a stigma even to-day. It makes it harder than ever for people to cope with the problems it causes. Still, it makes it even more im-perative that I find a place to live and get out of their way.' James tossed the grass into the hedge. 'That being the case, how about you taking pity on a poor lost soul and showing me the way?'

'Well...' Elizabeth hesitated, her reluctance plain to see in her hazel eyes. After all, hadn't she planned this day as a 'James-free' time specifically so that she could get the situation straight in her mind? What point was there in spending time with him when it only made her feel more confused?

'Of course, you've probably made plans already. Sorry, Beth, I didn't mean to put you on the spot like that.'

Was it the use of that diminutive again which sud-denly decided her? Or the hint of regret she heard in his voice? Elizabeth refused to believe it was either. If she agreed, it was purely out of a desire to help a colleague in difficulty. It was something she would have done for anyone in such circumstances so why should she make him the exception? Maybe that was at the root of the problem—the fact that she wasn't making any effort to see James as just another colleague!

'I haven't anything actually planned. I was just out for a walk, in fact. If you want me to come with you, I will.'

'Great!' He reached out and gave her a quick hug. It was all over in a second, and then he moved away to pick up the haversack, lying by the gate, so there was little justification for the way her heart began to beat as though she'd just run the race of her life.

'Th-this way.' Rather giddily, Elizabeth led the way along the path, hearing the soft thud of James's footsteps following her. She took a deep breath and sent up a silent prayer that she hadn't been too hasty in casting aside her former plans for the day. All she wanted was to help a colleague in difficulty, she assured herself, but her reasoning fell on deaf ears.

Trying to confine James to the role of colleague had never seemed harder than it did at that moment!

'You have to be kidding! This can't be the place!'

James's voice echoed with disbelief but there again the smallest sound echoed inside the building! Elizabeth tried not to laugh but it was impossible when she saw the expression on his face.

The walk had done a lot to ease her mind. James had kept the conversation to purely impersonal topics so that after a while she'd begun to relax a little, enough at least to make it easy for her to enjoy his reaction now. 'Don't you like it? There are wonderful views from all the windows...and through the roof, of course!'

'Wonderful views... You wretch! You knew it was a ruin, didn't you? No wonder you thought it so funny that I wanted to see the place. I just can't believe that Harry sent me here!'

James groaned as he turned in a slow circle, studying what had once been the living-room of the cottage. Part of the roof had caved in, as Elizabeth had pointed out, leaving the place open to the elements. There were rust-brown stains on the peeling wallpaper where rain had run down the walls, and grass was growing out of the old iron fireplace. The place was a mess and she couldn't help laughing at the thought of James, living in such a run-down property.

'Not quite what you had in mind? Yet with a little work it could be turned into a very desirable residence.'

'A little work?' James retorted, moving cautiously towards the kitchen to peer inside. 'Nothing less than a total renovation will get this place straight!'

Elizabeth glanced at the sagging cupboards and the cracked porcelain sink with its buckled wooden draining-board and grinned. 'Mmm, I suppose it depends if you're into a spot of DIY, of course.'

'I know my limitations!' James shot a telling glance over his shoulder. 'Oh, I can splash on paint with the best but this sort of job is beyond me. Is that another black mark against me, Beth?'

'I'm sorry?' She frowned as she tried to work out what he meant.

'The fact that I can't turn my hand to a job like this?' He gave a teasing laugh as he leaned against the doorframe and regarded her with amused blue eyes. 'I imagine a *real* country GP should be able to cope with any and every eventuality, even doing up a place like this from scratch.'

She wasn't sure she enjoyed being teased like this, especially not in view of how she'd been feeling lately. Elizabeth summoned a cool smile, not liking how it made her feel to have James taunt her ever so gently with her own doubts.

'As long as a GP has the skill to attend to his patients' needs I don't think it counts if he isn't a dab hand at house-renovating,' she replied with a laugh that she'd meant to be light but which had gone down like a lead balloon.

'Hmm, so maybe I'm still in with a chance. You aren't going to hold this against me, then, Beth?' There was a sudden seriousness to the question, a new intentness to the look he gave her. Elizabeth turned away, not wanting to be drawn into such a pointless discussion. How could she explain her misgivings to him when she had such trouble understanding them herself?

He gave a heavy sigh as he moved out of the kitchen. 'Obviously, you prefer not to commit yourself just yet. Now, seeing as this bijou residence isn't quite what I'd had in mind, how about number two on that list? Is it far from here?'

He smiled but there was a suggestion of hurt in his eyes that made Elizabeth feel wretched. It wasn't like her not to give people a chance so why was she treating him differently?

'A couple of miles back the way we came. But this time we need to take the other fork in the path,' she explained quickly, because it made her uncomfortable to admit how oddly she was behaving. 'It should take about half an hour or so to get there, that's all.'

'Right, then, you lead and I'll follow.' James grimaced as he closed the cottage door. 'And let's hope the next place is in a better state than this!'

His tone was light enough but Elizabeth heard the undercurrent it still held. She sighed inwardly as they left the cottage. How simple life would be if she could just accept James as everyone else seemed to have done, but it seemed impossible to do that.

The sun grew hotter as they made their way back along the path. Elizabeth rolled up the sleeves of her sweatshirt, wishing that she'd chosen to wear something cooler. It was unusually warm for the time of year, the late April sun beating down on them as they walked. The path ran alongside the banks of Yewdale Water once they'd got back to the fork, and through a gap in the hedge she could see several yachts on the lake as people took advantage of the glorious day.

'How about stopping for something to eat?' James swung the haversack off his shoulder. 'I don't know about you but all this fresh air has given me an appetite.

Rose packed me some sandwiches. She must have had an idea I'd get lost!'

'Sounds good to me.' Elizabeth smiled, determined to keep things as normal as possible. 'Look, there's a gap in the hedge. We should be able to squeeze through there and then we can sit by the lake.'

James led the way, holding back the prickly branches while she wriggled through the gap. Stripping off his sweater, he tossed it onto the ground to form a makeshift blanket. 'There you go. Sit yourself down and I'll see what we've got to eat.' He began to unpack foil-wrapped sandwiches as she sat down. 'Ham, cheese, beef...and a couple of cans of Coke. Not bad.'

He offered her one of the packets and Elizabeth took a thick beef sandwich and bit into it, realising only then how hungry she was. They ate in silence as they watched the yachts skim over the lake, their brightly coloured sails making them look like exotic birds. When the last sandwich had been consumed James leaned back on his elbows with a sigh of contentment.

'I don't think I ever enjoyed a meal so much. It must be the fresh air.' He turned to look at her, his eyes screwed up against the sun. 'I can understand why you love this place, Elizabeth. Even after just a couple of weeks I already feel at home here.'

'Do you?' She gave a faintly sceptical laugh as she plucked at a blade of grass, wishing he hadn't said such a thing yet unable to let it pass. 'It's a bit soon to decide that, surely?'

'Meaning that you still think the novelty will wear off once the honeymoon period is over?' He grinned, seemingly unconcerned by her scepticism. Lying back on the grass, he shaded his eyes with a tanned forearm as he stared at the sky. 'I suppose it's possible. Doubtful, but possible. I'm willing to concede that. However, I think, come this time next year, I'll still feel the same. How about you, though?'

'What do you mean?' Elizabeth frowned at the sudden twist in the conversation.

'Can *you* guarantee that your feelings won't have changed in twelve months' time? People always try to plan for the future but—as you pointed out—so often you find that things don't turn out the way you expected them to.'

'Are you thinking about Harriet when you say that?' Elizabeth coloured, wondering why she'd brought the subject up again. However, James didn't appear concerned that she'd mentioned it.

'It certainly could apply to that situation. At one point it all seemed cut and dried to me—Harriet and I would move to Cumbria and make a life for ourselves here— only it didn't work out that way.' He rolled onto his side, propping his head on his hand as he regarded her thoughtfully.

'Still, maybe you're better at planning the future than most people. So, if things go according to plan, where do you see yourself in twelve months' time, Elizabeth? Do you think you and David will have got it together at last?'

'I...I don't know.' She started to gather up the crumpled foil, not happy with the question or how it made her feel to realise that she had no idea what the answer was.

'You don't know!' James gave a disbelieving laugh. 'That doesn't sound like you, Elizabeth. You always give the impression that you're so certain about everything. I can't believe that you haven't thought about the future—it doesn't fit the image I have of you.'

'I've no idea what you mean,' she said shortly, avoiding his gaze because it made her feel uneasy.

'All right, then, let me give you an example—what about working here? Did it ever cross your mind *not* to return to Yewdale once you were qualified?'

He made it sound as though she was so narrow-minded that she couldn't possibly have considered anything else! The thought stung although Elizabeth didn't give herself time to consider why it should do so. 'Yes, if you really want to know! At one point I was considering going into obstetrics.'

'Really? What made you change your mind?'

Too late she realised the hole she'd dug for herself. Elizabeth looked towards the lake, watching a flotilla of canoes setting off from the shore as she thought about the reason for her change of direction. How could she explain to James that it had been the ending of her one and only love affair which had sent her back to the security of Yewdale? Put like that, it sounded so…feeble, but it hadn't been that way at all!

Not that she'd ever regretted it, of course. She'd found everything she'd been looking for right here—peace and the security of knowing that never again would she run the risk of being hurt…

'Sometimes we need to take risks, Beth. It's the only way to find out what we really and truly want from life.'

James's tone was very gentle yet she felt the shock course through her as she realised that somehow he'd latched onto her thoughts. Her hazel eyes were bright with surprise as they rose to his face before she looked away, but in those few seconds she saw the understanding in his gaze. She deliberately kept her face averted as he continued in the same quiet tone which had the ability to disturb her so much.

'I don't know exactly what happened to make you change your mind about the career you had mapped out, but I can guess. Did it have something to do with a man?

Were you hurt so badly that you came back here to the one place where you felt safe?'

He paused and Elizabeth found herself holding her breath as she wondered what he might say next. She felt stunned by his astuteness, by the way he'd summed up her reasons so easily, but nothing could have prepared her as he went on in the same level tone which offered no concessions.

'Is that why you believe yourself in love with David? Because he doesn't threaten you on an emotional level?'

'No!' Elizabeth scrambled to her feet. Her heart was hammering hard. 'Just who do you think you are? You know nothing about what I do or don't feel for David or...or anyone else!'

'Don't I?' He stood as well. His eyes were suddenly hooded as he studied her. 'I've seen the way you act around David, Elizabeth. It's obvious that you're very fond of him, as he is of you, but that's as far as it goes. You don't behave as though you're madly, passionately, in love with him, that's for sure!'

'Just because...because I don't believe in wearing my heart on my sleeve doesn't mean I don't feel such things,' Elizabeth retorted hotly. 'David has been through a lot in the past two years. If I behave... discreetly it's because I don't want to put him under any kind of pressure!'

'Is it? Sounds very noble to me, but maybe you should take a long, hard look at the situation. You might find it isn't quite what you thought it to be.' He laughed shortly. 'And that bit of advice comes straight from the heart. If I'd had the sense to take a hard look at my own situation I would have done things differently, believe me!'

'And probably not been fool enough to ruin your relationship with Harriet, by accepting this partnership? Is that what you mean, James?' Elizabeth laughed shrilly, stung by that thought. 'Well, you know what the answer is, don't you?'

'Call it quits at the end of the three months and go back to London?' He shook his head so that the sunlight glinted off his fair hair. 'There is no chance of that happening, Elizabeth.'

He bent and picked up his sweater, shaking off the bits of grass before packing it into the haversack along with the empty cans and foil. 'Right, that's that. How far is it to the other house on that list now?'

'Not very far.' Elizabeth took a long breath, although why she should let James get to her like this was beyond her. She pointed towards the path as she struggled for control. 'Carry on along there until you come to a stone cottage with blue-painted window-frames. If you turn sharp right the house is just down that lane. It's actually next door to David's house.'

'Is it? That's a coincidence.' James hefted the bag onto his shoulder, pausing as she made no attempt to accompany him back to the path. 'Are you coming?'

Elizabeth shook her head. 'No, I'd better get back. There are a few things I need to do,' she invented. It had been a mistake to come with him. She saw that now it was too late to do anything about it!

'Fair enough. Thanks for the company, Elizabeth. I've enjoyed it…despite our little disagreement.' He walked towards the gap in the hedge then paused to glance back. 'Oh, if I see David I'll give him your love, shall I?'

There was a wicked gleam in his blue eyes, a hint of mockery in the laugh he gave. Elizabeth had no time to come up with a reply, however, before he uttered a rough exclamation. 'What the devil…?'

Surprised, she turned to see what he was looking at and felt her heart leap into her throat as she took in the

scene. The canoes she'd noticed earlier were some way
out from the shore now. Elizabeth guessed that it was a
group from the Outward Bound centre because she could
see a couple of instructors paddling towards one canoe
which seemed to be having difficulty in keeping upright.
They seemed oblivious to the fact that there was a yacht
bearing down on them.

'If he doesn't tack soon he's going to run right into
them!' James grated. He'd no sooner spoken than it became obvious that some of the party had spotted the
danger for themselves. Pandemonium broke out suddenly as canoes started to scatter in all directions.
Elizabeth watched in horror as several collided and
promptly rolled over in the water.

'Come on!' James started racing towards the lake.
Elizabeth followed as fast as she could but she had no
hope of keeping up as his long legs covered the distance
in half the time it took her. By the time she got to the
shore some of the canoeists had already scrambled out
of the water and were standing about, looking under-
standably shaken.

Shading her eyes against the glare, she stared towards
the lake. The yacht had capsized now as well. Its mast
had landed squarely on top of one overturned canoe, its
red sail almost hiding it from view. Both instructors were
paddling frantically about, helping members of the party
to right themselves and directing them back to shore.
They seemed unaware that one canoe was still floating
upside down and that whoever was in it was trapped
under water.

'That kid's going to drown if someone doesn't get him
out fast!' Even as he spoke, James was kicking off his
trainers. He shot a glance at Elizabeth, 'Get one of this
lot to phone for an ambulance, Beth. Now!'

Before she could reply he'd waded into the water. He

struck out in a fast crawl, heading straight for the over-turned canoe. The instructors had spotted it now because they both turned and started paddling furiously towards it, but James got there ahead of them. Elizabeth's heart was in her mouth as she watched from the shore. How long had the canoeist been under water—two minutes, three?

She turned to one of the teenagers, realising only as she shot out instructions that it was Nick, the boy they'd helped the previous Saturday. This was one holiday he'd remember! 'Run back to the centre and call an ambulance. And let Mr Farnsworth know what's happened!'

The boy shot a frightened glance over his shoulder before he raced away. Elizabeth turned to watch what was happening and gasped in horror as she saw James dive and suddenly disappear beneath the hull of the canoe. The ensuing wait seemed agonisingly long as the seconds ticked past. Suddenly he reappeared, supporting the limp form of the canoeist.

Both instructors had reached them now. Elizabeth watched as they took hold of the youngster between them and started back to shore. She waded into the water, along with several others from the party, and helped to lift the girl onto the beach.

'Put her down there—quickly!' Elizabeth instructed once they'd got her clear of the water. She checked the girl's vital signs rapidly, but there was no breathing and no sign of a pulse so she wasted no time in starting the resuscitation procedure.

Checking that the girl's airway was clear, Elizabeth started CPR with mouth-to-mouth ventilation. Four sharp breaths were followed by fifteen chest compressions—vital to get the oxygen circulating through the girl's body and prevent brain damage. Elizabeth forced herself to concentrate solely on what she was doing, not allowing herself to wonder if James was all right. It was such a long swim back to shore, and the water was so cold...

She clamped down on the scene that flashed before her mind's eye and focused once more on the girl, automatically checking for a pulse before carrying on when she found none. The rest of the canoeing party stood around silently, shocked by the tragedy which had struck them out of the blue.

'I'll take over here, Dr Allen.' One of the instructors crouched down beside Elizabeth. He waited until she'd breathed into the girl's mouth then slipped into her place and carried on with the chest compressions as Elizabeth moved aside. 'Can you go and take a look at the fellow off the yacht? Dr Sinclair's just got him back to shore.'

Elizabeth got to her feet shakily, trembling from the exertion of keeping up the resuscitation for what had seemed a long time. She hurried over to where James was kneeling next to a middle-aged man, wearing a fluorescent orange life-jacket. The man's face was contorted with pain but somehow he managed to speak.

'How is she? I didn't see them until it was too late, you see. I tried to turn but I've only been out on the yacht once before—' He broke off with a groan as he clutched his left arm.

'He's got a broken arm,' James said quietly. 'Take a look, will you?'

Elizabeth knelt, gently feeling the man's upper arm. 'Yes, you're right. It's definitely a displaced fracture of the humerus.'

'I thought so. I don't want to run the risk of the radial nerve being damaged so can you get one of the kids to fetch a first-aid kit? I'll immobilise it until the ambulance gets here.'

'Of course.' Elizabeth stood up then hesitated. She

couldn't explain how she felt at that moment, didn't try to understand it even. 'You…you *are* all right, James?'

'I'm fine, Beth.' He gave her a slow smile, his eyes holding a wealth of emotion as he added softly, 'There's no need to worry about me.'

She turned and hurried back to the girl, trying not to wonder why there seemed to be a warm glow in the region of her heart or a feeling of excitement in her veins. There would be time enough later to work through the jumble of emotions she felt. For now it was enough to know that James was safe…

CHAPTER NINE

'How is she? Has there been any response yet?' Elizabeth knelt beside the instructors, who were now both working to resuscitate the girl.

'She was under the water a hell of a long time...' Ted Davies, the senior instructor, looked grim as he bent to breathe into her mouth.

'I know, but the water in there is very cold at this time of the year and that would have worked for her. There's a response to being immersed in very cold water known as the diving reflex, which maintains a minimal blood supply to the brain—' She broke off as the girl suddenly gasped and began to cough up water.

'That's it! Quick, put her on her side so that she can get rid of that water. And will someone fetch a blanket, please?'

By the time the ambulance arrived the girl was conscious again. Her name was Emma and the chance to learn how to canoe had been the main reason she'd wanted to come on the adventure weekend, it turned out. She got quite upset at the idea of going to hospital, but after Elizabeth had explained that it was necessary to avoid any later complications she quietened down.

The ambulance crew got her settled, then loaded the yachtsman on board as well. It was obvious he was in a great deal of pain and James was administering an injection of pethidine when Ian Farnsworth arrived with the local police, who wanted to take statements from everyone involved in the incident.

'I don't think either of them are up to giving a statement at the moment,' James put in firmly as he got out of the ambulance. 'It's imperative that Emma is taken to hospital straight away. Although she seems to have come through remarkably well, there's always the danger that water has collected in her lungs, which could lead to pulmonary oedema. The sooner she's given a thorough check-up the happier I'll be.'

The police obviously saw the wisdom of this, making no objection as the ambulance drove off. They took statements from everyone else, though. Ian Farnsworth shook his head as James repeated what the yachtsman had said about it having been only the second time he'd been out in the boat.

'People don't take enough care around water. When you think how long it takes to learn to drive a car and yet they have a couple of lessons and think they know all there is to know about sailing! Every year you get folks being hurt or killed because they don't weigh up the risks.'

'At least everything turned out all right today,' Elizabeth said.

'Only because there were people around who were trained to deal with this sort of emergency. And heaven knows what would have happened if James hadn't managed to get Emma out of that canoe.' Ian held out his hand. 'Thank you. It makes me go cold to think that I might have had to phone the girl's parents to tell them that their daughter was dead if you hadn't been so quick to act.'

There didn't seem a lot anyone could say after that. It was a very subdued group of youngsters that started to make its way back to the centre. Ian offered to run Elizabeth and James back to town in the van, but they refused. He had enough to do to comfort the children and phone Emma's parents, without worrying about them.

'Well, that's that.' James sighed as he glanced towards the lake. 'Hard to believe that a near tragedy could happen on a day like this, isn't it?'

'It is. But, then, that's usually the case. Things tend to happen when you least expect them to,' Elizabeth agreed.

'You're right.' He turned to look at her and there seemed to be a new depth to his voice as he quietly endorsed the sentiment. 'You never know what's going to happen, do you?'

Elizabeth told herself that it was her imagination that seemed to imbue the words with an extra dimension. 'You certainly don't. Now, I think we'd better get back. It might be a lovely day but the water in that lake is freezing even in the middle of summer. You'll catch a chill if you don't get out of those wet clothes soon.'

The nervousness she felt was reflected in the high pitch of her voice, and she saw James shoot her a considering look. He didn't say anything, however, but simply followed her as she led the way back to the path.

Elizabeth took a long, slow breath and let it out even more slowly, but she couldn't rid herself of the feeling that something momentous had happened. What was it? Even as she asked herself the question she shied away from the answer. Maybe it was safer not to go delving too deeply into things she didn't understand...

By the time they reached Yewdale House James was blue with cold. Elizabeth shot him an anxious look and made up her mind there and then what had to be done.

'You'd better come in. You need to get out of those wet things straight away. You look half-frozen.'

'Well, if you don't mind...' James managed a grin,

despite the fact that his teeth were clattering away like castanets. 'You weren't kidding when you said that water was cold! I don't think I'll be rushing into it again.'

'Let's hope you don't have to.' There was a shaky note in her voice she couldn't quite disguise. She quickly led the way up the path, not wanting James to see how much it bothered her to recall how he'd disappeared beneath the water.

The key grated in the lock before she managed to open the door. She stepped inside the hall and looked around at all the comfortingly familiar things as she tried to wipe the picture from her mind, but it wouldn't seem to go...

'It's OK, Beth. Everything turned out all right.'

James's voice was soothing and she managed a smile as she turned to him, not even wondering this time how he'd read her mind. He had this ability to know what she was thinking and no amount of wondering how or why would alter that.

'Yes, you're right. It could have been a lot worse, couldn't it?' She forced herself to concentrate on practicalities, knowing that was the best way to deal with what had happened. 'Now, why don't you go upstairs and have a hot shower? That should warm you up. And I'm sure I can find some clothes of my father's if you don't mind wearing them.'

'Thanks. Anything dry will do. It will be better than having to trail back to town, looking like a drowned rat!' James accepted the offer with a grin that helped to wipe away any lingering echoes of the traumatic incident. Elizabeth laughed with him, suddenly more at ease.

'I imagine that depends on what I can find! My father isn't exactly known for his sartorial elegance. Anyway, go and have that shower. The bathroom's the first door on the left at the top of the stairs. Dad's bedroom is next to it so I'll lay out some clothes on the bed for you. I'll just put a pot of coffee on first. I think we could both do with a cup.'

Leaving James to make his way up to the bathroom, Elizabeth went to the kitchen and measured coffee into the percolator. She left it to brew then hurried upstairs. It was difficult to find anything to fit James because her father was a good deal shorter—and wider—than James, but eventually she dug out a pair of elderly trousers and a check shirt and laid them on the bed.

'Would you mind taking a look at my shoulder, Beth?'

She hadn't realised that the shower had stopped, and swung round as she heard his voice. She felt her heart stop before it started to race wildly as she saw him, standing in the doorway. In a fast sweep her eyes drank in the sight he made, clad only in a white towel wrapped around his narrow hips. There were beads of moisture on his skin, diamond-bright droplets caught in the thick tangle of golden hair that covered his muscular chest and thighs.

Elizabeth found her eyes drawn to them, to the way they glittered as they caught the light from the window...

'Beth?' There was a rough timbre to his voice which jolted her back to the present. She took a deep breath, her heart still pounding crazily and her blood racing.

'Your shoulder?' she queried, then cleared her throat as she heard the huskiness in her voice. 'Have you hurt it?'

'I think I may have scraped it on the hull of the canoe.' He turned so she could see the angry red graze across his shoulder-blade, and Elizabeth dragged her thoughts into some semblance of order.

'Oh, yes. It...it looks rather nasty. I think I'd better

put something on it. I'll just get my bag.' Her voice sounded so strange still that it might not have belonged to her. She hurried from the room, not wanting to look at James and see if he was aware of it. It took only minutes to go downstairs and find her bag, but in that short time he'd put on the trousers and had made his way to the kitchen.

Elizabeth followed him into the room and laid her case on the table, busying herself with getting out what she needed—antiseptic and some sterile gauze dressings. It seemed safer to concentrate on that rather than to let her imagination run riot again, wondering how it would feel to touch that smooth warm skin...feel the crispness of hair beneath her fingers...

'I'll just clean the cut first to make sure there's nothing in it,' she informed him quickly, clamping down on such wayward thoughts.

She poured a little antiseptic solution onto a sterile pad and wiped it over the graze as gently as she could, but she still felt him flinch.

'Ouch! That stings!' He turned to cast a mock-reproachful glance over his shoulder at the exact moment that she bent to check that the cut was completely clean. Their mouths brushed, clung for one second, two—

Elizabeth drew back abruptly. The colour rushed to her face and her heart pounded so loudly she thought he must be able to hear it. 'I'm sorry...' she began.

'Don't be!' He gave a smoky laugh as he lifted his hand to cup the back of her head and drew her towards him again. 'That's the sort of accident I enjoy dealing with!'

His mouth was so gentle as it covered hers that Elizabeth felt herself melt instantly. Deep down she knew that she should stop what was happening but she found it impossible to resist the drug-like sweetness of his lips as they clung to hers. Her breath escaped on a tiny sigh of pure pleasure as she returned his kiss. She felt him tense before his lips parted to deepen the kiss—

'I'm back! Oh, it's been a lovely day. Robert was so pleased to see me, too.'

The sound of Mrs Lewis's cheery voice broke the spell with a speed that made Elizabeth's head reel. There was a moment when James's lips clung to hers, as though he couldn't bear to break away, before he let her go and stood up just as the housekeeper appeared in the doorway.

'Why, Dr Sinclair, I'd no idea you were coming round this afternoon.' Mrs Lewis looked faintly startled as she took in the fact that he was half-dressed. Her eyes flew from him to Elizabeth and back again as he gave a rueful laugh.

'Neither had I, Mrs Lewis! It definitely wasn't on the agenda when I set off this morning, but there was a sudden change of plans, you might say.' He picked up the shirt from the back of the chair and shrugged it on.

Elizabeth took a quick breath, knowing that she had to say something by way of explanation. 'There was an accident at the lake. Dr Sinclair and I happened to be there at the time and we helped out. I insisted he came back and changed out of his wet clothes.'

It was such a mundane explanation and it didn't even touch on how she felt, her mind and body in turmoil as she thought about that kiss...

Elizabeth dragged her mind back to what was happening as Mrs Lewis gave a horrified gasp. 'An accident, you say? But whatever happened? Nobody was hurt, I hope!'

It was James who explained quietly what had gone on, carefully playing down his own role in it. Elizabeth listened to his voice as though she were hearing it at one step removed. She felt oddly detached from what was happening. All she could think about was how James had kissed her, how...how she had kissed him back!

'Beth?' There was a gentleness in his voice which brought her eyes winging to his face, and she felt herself colour as she saw the awareness there. 'I think I'd better go. Thanks for the clothes...and cleaning that cut for me.'

There was a nuance to the words which made her heart race. Elizabeth turned away, not needing to be reminded of what had happened. She led the way quickly from the kitchen and opened the front door, standing aside so that James could pass her. He paused in the doorway and there was an intentness to the look he gave her which served to heat her blood even more.

'I'm not going to apologise for what happened just now, Beth. I wouldn't insult either of us, by doing that.' His deep voice grated and Elizabeth shivered as she felt each and every syllable scrape against nerves already rawly sensitive. She kept her gaze averted, afraid to look at him and see what he was thinking. That kiss had been a mistake! She knew that even if he didn't. And an apology, or lack of one, didn't alter that!

He uttered something rough as he brought her head round so that he could look into her eyes. 'Damn it, Beth, you can't pretend it didn't happen!'

'I...I'm not trying to pretend anything!' Suddenly her anger surfaced, rising on the back of a feeling of helplessness she couldn't control. She gave a discordant laugh. 'Why should I? It didn't mean anything, James! It was just a kiss, the...the result of all the drama, that's all!'

'Think so?' He gave another of those disturbing, smoky laughs as he let her go. 'You could be right, Beth.

Maybe it was the drama of the situation which made it happen. After all, it's David you're in love with so there has to be an explanation as to why you let another man kiss you.'

He gave her a last slow smile before he walked out of the door. Elizabeth wanted to scream after him that nothing had changed, that she did love David, only she knew in her heart that the words might hold more desperation than conviction.

The next few days passed in a whirl. News of what had happened at the lake soon got around the town so that Elizabeth had no chance to put it out of her mind, as she wanted to do. It seemed that every patient she saw wanted to talk about it until she felt she'd scream if she had to answer any more questions.

The memory of that kiss plagued her. She found her thoughts going back to it constantly, although she steadfastly refused to allow herself to examine her feelings. It had happened and that was that. She had to accept it and get on with her life, but it wasn't easy to follow her own sensible advice!

It made her very self-conscious around James, but as the days passed and he made no mention of it she began to relax. Maybe James had realised that there'd been some truth in what she'd said, and that the kiss had been simply the result of their heightened emotions?

It made it easier to cope if she thought that, although in her heart Elizabeth knew it wasn't the real answer and that one day soon she'd have to face up to it.

A week passed and then another, and life settled into a regular pattern. Having James around was proving very beneficial…in some respects! Several projects which had had to be shelved were started up.

The family planning clinic, which Elizabeth had long

wanted to set up, finally got off the ground and she was delighted with the response. She'd decided to hold it after evening surgery so that any woman who was working during the day would have the chance to attend, and there were five appointments for the first session. Cathy Fielding was one of them.

'Hello, Cathy. Come in and sit down. I'm glad you could come.' Elizabeth smiled reassuringly, sensing the girl's nervousness. A pretty girl with dark hair and a lovely smile, Cathy worked at the local pottery, hand-painting some of the more expensive items produced there.

'Well, I thought I'd better, Dr Allen.' Cathy blushed. 'You see, me and Jim are going away on holiday this year—to Spain, in fact.'

'Jim? Jim Patterson, do you mean?' Elizabeth smiled. 'You two have been seeing each other for some time now, haven't you?'

'Yes.' Cathy blushed a bit more. 'Actually, Dr Allen, we've just got engaged. My mum and dad wouldn't have been happy about us going away together otherwise,' she added, holding out her hand so that Elizabeth could see the tiny diamond solitaire she was wearing.

'Congratulations!' Elizabeth said, delighted by the news. 'And I think it's very sensible of you to come to the clinic before you go away. You don't want any little surprises after you come home, do you?'

Cathy laughed but there was still a hint of embarrassment in her voice. 'That's right, Dr Allen. Oh, I know me and Jim intend to get married but we don't want to, well, have to rush things.' She avoided Elizabeth's eyes. 'So far we haven't... Well, we just haven't...you know?'

'I understand, Cathy, and there's really no need to be embarrassed. I think you've been right to wait until you're absolutely certain it's what you want. Now, I just want to check a few things—blood pressure, weight, things like that. Then we can discuss what methods of contraception you might prefer.'

By the time Cathy was ready to leave she was looking a lot more relaxed. Elizabeth had ended up prescribing a form of the minipill for her as it seemed the most suitable. She made sure that Cathy understood that she must take it at exactly the same time each day for it to be effective, and what she should do if she happened to suffer any tummy troubles while she was in Spain! However, she knew how sensible the girl was, and was confident that she wouldn't have any problems.

'Thank you, Dr Allen. I was dreading coming, to tell the truth, but it wasn't half so bad as I thought.' Cathy turned to leave, then paused. 'Oh, by the way, could you write me out a prescription for some more of that cream for my psoriasis? It would save me having to come back to the surgery after work, if you wouldn't mind.'

'Of course not.' Elizabeth checked Cathy's notes and quickly wrote out a repeat prescription. Cathy had suffered from the skin complaint for a number of years now, and trial and error had proved this cream to be the most effective. 'How has it been lately?'

'So-so.' Cathy grimaced as she pushed up her sleeve so that Elizabeth could see the scaly red patches on her elbow. 'It comes and goes, as you know, but I want to try to get rid of it before we go away. I don't want people staring at me when I go for a swim!'

'It isn't contagious,' Elizabeth said consolingly, 'so there's no need to worry about anyone catching it off you.'

'Oh, I know that but other people don't and it looks ugly. I only wish I could find something to shift it once and for all.'

'Unfortunately, psoriasis does tend to recur, but I could arrange for you to see a consultant if you'd like. He might be able to suggest something different,' Elizabeth offered sympathetically.

'But that would mean going all the way to the hospital, wouldn't it?' Cathy shook her head. 'They don't like you taking time off work unless it's for something really urgent.'

'We're toying with the idea of setting up a video link between the surgery and the hospital, then you could speak to a consultant just by coming in here. How would you feel about that?' Elizabeth queried, faintly surprised that she'd raised the matter.

'That it was a brilliant idea! It's all the time it takes to get to the hospital that's the problem, isn't it? You'll let me know when it's up and running, won't you?'

'Of course.' Elizabeth sighed as Cathy left. Maybe she'd been too quick to decry James's suggestion but, then, she'd hardly dealt with his advent in Yewdale in her usual logical manner. Where James was concerned, logic seemed to take second place!

That was too disquieting to think about so Elizabeth turned her mind to her work and finished the rest of her appointments. She was getting ready to lock up when there was a tap on the door and a young girl appeared.

'Have you got a minute, Dr Allen? I know it's late...'

'It doesn't matter. Come in. It's Sophie Jackson, isn't it?' Elizabeth queried because it had been some time since she'd seen the Jacksons' oldest daughter.

'Yes, that's right,' Sophie came into the room and stood awkwardly by the desk.

'Why don't you sit down, Sophie?' Elizabeth waited until the girl had perched on the edge of the chair. She was obviously upset about something to judge by the way she sat there, twisting a lock of lank brown hair.

She was dressed in jeans and a bulky knit jumper, which must have been hot on such a mild evening.

Elizabeth gave her a moment, then realised that Sophie wasn't going to say anything without being prompted. 'So, what brings you here tonight, Sophie?' She paused. 'You aren't here for the family planning clinic, are you?'

'Not really,' Sophie muttered as she bit at her thumb-nail. 'It's a bit late for that, you see, Dr Allen.'

'A bit late...?' It took Elizabeth a second to under-stand, and she had to struggle to hide her dismay. 'You mean you think you might be pregnant, Sophie?'

'Uh-huh. I think I must be.' Sophie looked up and there was panic in her eyes all of a sudden. 'I never meant it to happen! Honestly, I didn't! I don't know what Mum's going to do when she finds out. She's that worried about our Chloe, and what with having to trail to the hospital on the bus all the time and look after my brothers who are real pains—'

'I think the best thing we can do at the moment is to concentrate on you,' Elizabeth cut in, to stop the hys-terical outburst. 'We need to know how far on you are for starters so pop behind that screen and I'll examine you. Then we'll take things from there.'

From what Elizabeth could tell from the answers Sophie gave her, plus her own examination, the girl was about four months pregnant. Apart from an understand-able fear of what her parents were going to say, she seemed in excellent health.

Elizabeth tried to encourage Sophie to tell her parents before she made any decisions about what she intended to do, but she wasn't sure she'd succeeded when Sophie left. She sighed as she went through to Reception to write up the girl's notes, wondering how Annie and Barry were going to react when they found out. Sophie was only sixteen so the prospect of a baby at her age was hardly something they'd welcome—

'Penny for them?'

She jumped at the sound of that deep voice, swinging round so fast that she almost collided with James who was standing behind her.

'Careful!' James steadied her with a firm grip on her shoulders. He let her go as soon as he was sure that she was steady, but there was a look in his eyes which made her heart thunder. Why did she have the feeling that he didn't *want* to let her go? She had no idea, but just to think about it made a wash of heat run through her veins.

'Sorry. I didn't mean to startle you, Beth.' His deep voice grated, and she felt the heat spread through her whole body as she heard the awareness it held. James knew as well as she did that it wasn't just surprise which had caused her to react to his presence!

'I didn't realise you were here,' she said huskily, to cover her confusion.

'I wanted to drop these off.' He dropped a bundle of cards into the basket for Eileen to file the following day. 'They're the notes from the calls I did this afternoon. I left them in my bag by mistake. There wasn't anything very urgent but I thought I'd better bring them back in case Sam needed them tonight. How did you get on this evening? Did you have many takers for your first session?'

'Five, which was quite good.' Elizabeth struggled to keep her tone level. 'I've been wanting to set up this clinic for some time as I've long felt there was a need for it.' She sighed. 'Although it was a shade too late for one of my visitors tonight—Sophie Jackson.'

'Annie's daughter?' James frowned. 'She can't be more than sixteen. Did she want family planning advice? And what do you mean about it being too late?'

'Guess!' Elizabeth ran a hand through her hair, ruffling the glistening auburn strands so that they curled around her cheeks. She saw a strange expression across James's face but couldn't understand what had caused it.

She hurried on, aware that her heart was beating painfully fast. 'Sophie is four months pregnant, it turns out.'

'Really?' James whistled softly. 'And do her parents know?' He grimaced when she shook her head. 'What a mess, eh? Annie could do without this on top of everything else.' He glanced at his watch and sighed. 'Well, I suppose I'd better let you get on. It's been a long day for you, Beth. You must be tired. The clinic's a great idea but it means you working extra hours, doesn't it?'

'I don't mind.' Elizabeth smiled, touched by the concern she heard in his voice. 'I'll put my feet up after I've had something to eat.'

'Mmm, that's exactly what I was thinking of doing. Mind you, I fancy a change from pub food, to tell the truth. Don't get me wrong. Rose is great cook, but it does tend to be chips with everything,' he said with a laugh.

'I was going to make myself an omelette. Would you like to join me?' Elizabeth offered before she thought about what she was saying.

'Do you mean that?' James turned to look at her and she felt her pulse leap as she saw the expression in his eyes, a mixture of surprise and real pleasure at the invitation.

'Of course,' she replied lightly, trying to hide the sudden nervousness she felt. 'Mrs Lewis has gone to a church social so you'll have to make do with my cooking. You've been warned!'

'I'm willing to risk it!' James laughed, his tone full

of a warmth which made her feel slightly dizzy. She hurried down the corridor ahead of him and let them into the house, going straight to the kitchen to take what she needed out of the fridge before she had time to re-consider the wisdom of what she was doing.

'Can I do anything to help?' James stood in the door-way, looking big and handsome as he stood there, watch-ing her, so that her pulse skipped a breath or two more.

'No, I can manage, thank you. You...you go and make yourself comfortable. It won't take long.'

He disappeared along the hall and Elizabeth let out her pent-up breath as she heard him opening the sitting-room door. She broke eggs into a bowl and chopped up some mushrooms and ham, concentrating on preparing the supper rather than thinking about James in the next room.

While the omelette was cooking she tossed together a salad then loaded everything onto a tray. James must have heard her coming along the hall because he jumped up and took the tray from her, waiting patiently while she drew a small table over in front of the sofa.

Mrs Lewis had left a fire burning and the room was cosy in the flickering glow from its flames. Night had started to draw in so Elizabeth went and drew the long velvet curtains across the windows while James set the tray down. The soft rose pink velvet had faded in places but still added to the overall feeling of cosiness which seemed to pervade the room.

'This is great.' James sank back on the sofa with a sigh of pleasure. 'I can't tell you how wonderful it is to sit here in peace and quiet for a change. It gets really busy at the pub most nights. I tried suggesting that I eat in my room but Harry was concerned about me being on my own.'

He laughed ruefully as she sat down beside him.

'Harry seems to think it's his duty to keep me enter-
tained while I'm staying there!'

Elizabeth smiled as she handed him a plate. 'Harry is
a very gregarious person, which is why running that pub
suits him down to the ground. But I know what you
mean. Sometimes it's nice just to have a few quiet
minutes on your own after a busy day, isn't it?'

'Or to share them with someone who understands that
you don't always need to keep up a constant conversation.'

James's voice was resonant as he looked at her.
Elizabeth struggled to find something to say but it was
impossible when she saw the message in his eyes.

Did he believe that she was that sort of a person,
someone he could sit with in quiet contemplation? In the
light of their past disagreements it seemed incredible to
think that he'd directed that comment at her, but she
knew he had. Despite everything, there *was* a bond of
understanding between them, and it shook her to realise
it.

They ate in silence, the gentle sputtering of the fire
the only accompaniment to the meal. James laid down
his knife and fork and sat back with a groan of contentment. 'That was delicious, Beth. You make a great
omelette, and if you ever need a reference I'll be happy
to give you one!'

Elizabeth laughed as she collected the plates and put
them on the tray. 'Thank you. I'm a dab hand at scrambled eggs as well. Oh, and poached, too, but that's where
my culinary expertise stops, I'm afraid. Now, how about
coffee?'

'Please. Here, let me take that.' Ignoring her protest,
James took the tray from her and carried it to the kitchen.
He put it next to the sink then turned on the taps, holding

up his hand when she opened her mouth. 'No, you cooked so the least I can do is wash up. It's only fair.'

'Is that how you and Harriet used to divide up the jobs?' Elizabeth gasped in dismay as she realised what she'd said. 'Sorry, it's none of my business...' she began, but James stopped her. There was something in his eyes which made her heart pound, though not with embarrassment this time. Why did she get the impression that he was *pleased* she'd asked such a question? It didn't make sense!

'Harriet and I weren't in often enough to worry about who did what. She's a very social person and prefers to go out to eat with her friends. I doubt we spent more than half a dozen evenings together in the flat the whole time we lived there.' James added washing-up liquid to the bowl and dunked the plates into the suds, grimacing as he suddenly realised that his shirtsleeves were in danger of getting soaked. 'Would you mind, Beth...?'

He held up his wet hands and automatically Elizabeth went over to roll up his sleeves for him. Her head was whirling as she tried to picture the kind of life he and Harriet had led. James must have found it very tiring, going out every night after a busy day at work, surely?

She frowned as she concentrated on working the tiny pearl buttons on his cuffs free and jumped when James said softly, 'A lot of the time I stayed in and let Harriet go out and do her own thing. It was easier.'

'Easier?' Her voice was so low that it barely disturbed the silence. She saw James smile as her eyes rose to his face and stayed there, held by the tenderness she saw in his gaze.

'Than arguing about it. It never seemed worth arguing about, Beth. But I only realised why recently.'

She wasn't sure what he meant and it was impossible to work it out when her mind was running this way and

that, reacting to his nearness in a way that made it hard
to think at all. She heard him laugh softly and looked
away, concentrating fiercely on undoing the cuffs of his
shirt.

The buttons popped free at last and she rolled up the
sleeves out of harm's way, trying not to notice how
warm his skin felt as her fingers brushed against it—but
that was like trying not to notice that the sun was shining
after a frost. Suddenly her whole body seemed suffused
with heat and she moved out of the way quickly as
James set about washing the dishes with a vigour which
hardly seemed warranted, considering the meal they'd
had.

They had coffee in the kitchen and James seemed to
go out of his way to keep the conversation light, for
which Elizabeth was grateful until it struck her that he
must have sensed how on edge she was. It was almost
a relief when he pushed back his chair and stood up.

'Well, it's been lovely, Beth, but I mustn't outstay my
welcome. How about letting me return the compliment?
I've offered to visit Chloe on Saturday to give Annie a
break—would you like to come with me? I know Chloe
would love to see you and, as an added inducement, I'll
treat you to lunch to say thank you for tonight.'

'There's no need—' Elizabeth began.

'I know there isn't. I know that you fed me tonight
out of the pure goodness of your heart!' James grinned
wickedly. 'But if you don't want to come it's OK. I
understand.'

Did he? Did he *really* understand how nervous she
felt at the prospect of spending time alone with him?
Did he understand *why* she felt like that when she wasn't
sure herself?

The thought stung. Elizabeth drew herself up, determined not to let him know how the idea disturbed her.

'Of course I'll come. I'd like to see Chloe, and I did promise to visit her.'

'Great!' James gave her a broad smile which did nothing to set her mind at rest. He looked a little like the cat who'd just been handed the biggest dish of cream...

Elizabeth refused point blank to pursue that line of thought! She followed him down the hall, waiting while he collected his jacket from the sitting-room. He stopped by the front door and his eyes seemed very deep and blue suddenly as they rested on her.

'Thanks for tonight, Beth. I enjoyed it.' He bent and kissed her lightly on the cheek, his lips lingering no longer than a single heartbeat, yet Elizabeth felt her head reel.

She stared at him with wide eyes and saw the look of tenderness that crossed his face. Reaching out, he placed the tip of one finger on the spot where his lips had been, and his touch was so gentle that she shivered. 'I've always known that this was the job for me, Beth, but now I'm more convinced than ever that I've found what I was looking for.'

He left without another word. Elizabeth closed the door and took a long, slow breath to quell the rush of excitement she felt. If she set her mind to it she could come up with any number of answers as to what James had meant by that statement...although the most tantalising one of all didn't take *any* thinking about!

Was James glad that he'd come to Yewdale because he had met her?

She closed her eyes. Maybe that *did* need thinking about after all!

CHAPTER TEN

'HELLO, I'm Laura Mackenzie, Chloe's consultant. She's been chattering away non-stop since she found out you were both coming to visit her today!'

Elizabeth took an immediate liking to the pretty blonde woman who greeted them outside the ward. She must have been in her mid-thirties, the colourful floral dress she was wearing accentuating a trimly curvaceous figure. Laura must have noticed her taking stock because she laughed softly.

'White coats are taboo around here! The children respond better if we just wear our everyday clothes. We try to keep things as casual as possible, you understand, so that the younger ones aren't overawed by it all.' She grimaced. 'It's enough for them having to cope with their treatment, without being scared of us as well.'

'It must make it easier for them,' Elizabeth agreed, glancing into the brightly painted ward. There were colourful pictures on all the walls, obviously drawn by the children, and heaps of toys piled up in the activity corner. Instead of the usual regulation white line, each bed sported brightly patterned sheets and covers to make them feel even more at home.

There were a dozen children in all in the ward, many of them hooked up to drips which were steadily feeding them the drugs they needed. However, even that didn't seem to slow them down all that much, she noticed, watching one little boy whizzing across the ward with his drip-stand in tow!

'So, how is Chloe doing, Dr Mackenzie?' James

asked. Elizabeth felt a tremor of awareness ripple down her spine at the sound of his voice and fought to control it.

She'd managed this far, she told herself sternly, kept up a conversation with him on the drive here and handled the visit with cool aplomb even if it was only on the surface. That underneath she was a churning mass of nerves was by the by. James wasn't going to find that out—not if she had anything to do with it!

'Laura, please!' She led them into the office and closed the door. She poured them all coffee then sat at the desk and sighed. 'We had a bit of setback when Chloe was first admitted. She started with a rather nasty chest infection so we had to delay her treatment.'

'I imagine it was too risky when it meant she'd have no resistance against the infection?' James hazarded quietly.

'That's right. We didn't dare start the chemotherapy until we'd managed to clear up her chest, which was a blow. We had to keep her in a side-ward as well because of the risk to the other children in the ward so she was a bit upset about that. However, now that the infection has cleared up we were able to start her on the drugs yesterday, and she'll be having a transfusion of blood and platelets soon.'

'What is the outlook for her?' Elizabeth asked.

'That's something we can never be sure of at this stage. We're aiming for remission, but that's many weeks away as yet. Then we'll consider a bone-marrow transplant, assuming that we find a suitable donor. Of course, it helps that Chloe is part of a large family as we have a far better chance of finding a donor with a similar tissue type to hers,' Laura explained.

'There's a twenty-five per cent chance of any brother or sister being compatible so, in Chloe's case, it means there are four times that same chance of finding the match. I'll arrange for blood samples to be taken from the family in the next week or so.'

'How much bone marrow do you need for a successful transplant?' James asked with interest.

'Surprisingly little—between twenty and fifty millilitres is all it takes. As you know, the patient's own bone marrow has to be eradicated to destroy the diseased cells. However, the transplanted marrow grows very rapidly and soon fills up the space in the bones so that isn't a problem. It's the possibility of rejection that's always the biggest headache,' Laura answered.

'Even when you have a good match?' Elizabeth queried.

'Yes, even then. GVHD, or graft-versus-host disease, is a huge problem. The lymphocytes in the donor marrow are able to tell they're in alien territory, so to speak. We use immunosuppressive drugs to prevent and treat rejection, but complications can and do occur for some time after the transplant takes place.' Laura smiled.

'However, it's something we're prepared for. As far as Chloe is concerned, all I can say is that we're achieving excellent results with children her age.'

She stood up. 'Now, if you've finished your coffee I'll take you in to see her. She'll be thrilled that her "Dr James" is here!'

Chloe was sitting up in bed, looking expectantly towards the door, when they went into the ward. Her small face broke into a delighted smile as she saw them. The words tumbled out as they reached her bed. 'I told everyone you'd come! Charlie and Jessica—that's her over there and she's my best friend—and Louise and Daniel—everyone!'

Elizabeth laughed as she perched on the edge of the

brightly covered bed. 'Sounds to me as though you know just about everyone in this ward!'

'I do!' Chloe grinned happily, despite the fact that she was attached to a drip which was feeding the life-saving drugs into her small body. 'I know all the children and all the nurses and doctors and the lady who brings our dinners. We had fish fingers and chips last night—and jelly!'

She turned to James, her face aglow as she looked at him. 'I've shown *everyone* my badge, Dr James. And *no one* has one like it!'

'That's because they aren't my very special patients, Chloe. You are.' He gave the small girl a gentle hug. The expression on his face brought a sudden lump to Elizabeth's throat. Such tenderness and caring, she thought, such genuine concern for this child.

Suddenly it was as though the scales had been torn from her eyes and she was seeing him clearly for the first time—without reservations, without inhibitions.

James Sinclair was a committed and caring doctor, a man who valued people and cared deeply about helping them. The fact that he'd chosen to come to this area to work when, materially, he could have expected so much more should have shown her that right from the beginning. It had been her own blindness, her own *fear*, which had closed her mind to that.

She was so shaken by the realisation that it was difficult to keep up the pretence that everything was all right as they spent the next half-hour at Chloe's bedside. When it became obvious that Chloe was tiring James rose and smiled at the little girl.

'I think we'd better go now, sweetheart. We don't want Dr Mackenzie telling us off for staying too long!'

Chloe giggled at the thought of anyone telling off her beloved Dr James, but she settled back against the pillows, her eyelids drooping. 'But you will come again, won't you? Both of you?'

James glanced at Elizabeth then reached out and took her hand in a gesture which was so natural that she felt no surprise. 'Yes, we'll come again...soon. Now, you have a little rest, Chloe. I expect your mummy and daddy will be here tomorrow to see you.'

''Spect so.' Chloe's thumb popped into her mouth as her eyes closed. They crept away from her bed, pausing briefly to have a word with Laura on their way out.

'I'm glad you could come. Chloe is such a sweet child and I know she's been looking forward to your visit.' Laura glanced across the ward, watching as a nurse in a bright red sweatshirt with a teddy-bear appliqueé on the front drew the curtains quietly around Chloe's bed. 'The drugs do tend to knock them out, especially the little ones. She'll sleep for a while now, I expect.'

'We'll come again soon, won't we, Beth?' James turned to her for confirmation and Elizabeth felt her heart melt as she saw the warmth in his eyes. James kept hold of her hand all the way to the car park, only letting it go so that he could open the car door for her.

'Thank you for coming, Beth. It meant a lot to Chloe...and to me.' His lips were gentle as swansdown as they settled on hers, but Elizabeth felt the surge her pulse gave. When he stepped back she had to stop herself from moving towards him again. She slid into the car, sitting stiffly as he started the engine.

They left the hospital and drove for a couple of miles before James turned through the gates of a restaurant set on the banks of the river. He'd reserved a table by the window for them, which gave a wonderful view of the river as it flowed past.

He turned to Elizabeth once they'd ordered, that same warmth still evident in his eyes. 'I promised you lunch, didn't I? I hope this place is all right. I found it by accident the other day and knew it would be the perfect place to bring you today.'

'It's lovely,' she said huskily, touched that he'd gone to so much trouble. Yet wasn't that just another indication of the kind of man he was?

She let her eyes play over his handsome face, seeing it with new eyes—each tiny line and wrinkle, each mark of character. She looked at him and saw him for what he was—a caring, compassionate, wonderfully tender man.

'I've been wrong about you, James.' Her voice was faint at first but grew in strength as she grasped her courage in both hands. 'Wrong to treat you the way I've been doing, wrong to…to have these doubts about you. I can see that now.'

'Can you?' His voice vibrated with emotion so that her hands clenched.

'Yes. I…I never gave you a chance to prove you meant what you'd said about wanting to work in Yewdale.' Her eyes were full of puzzlement as they met his. 'I don't know why, though. I've no idea why I've been acting that way.'

'Haven't you?' His tone was gentle as he reached out and brushed her mouth with his fingertips so that Elizabeth gasped. 'Are you sure about that, Beth?'

'I—' She got no further as the waiter arrived just then with their first course. The meal was delicious but Elizabeth barely tasted it. Every nerve in her body felt so tightly wound that she couldn't think of anything other than the tension that flowed between her and James.

'Would you like dessert?' he asked, once the waiter had cleared away their plates, but she shook her head. His eyes glittered with awareness, his voice dropping to a depth which made a shiver work its way down her spine. 'Coffee, perhaps?'

It was the sweetest kind of torment to know that he was teasing her with how they both felt. Elizabeth shook her head, her colour rising as she saw the flames that flared in his eyes before he turned to inform the waiter that they'd like their bill.

It seemed to take for ever before the essentials were sorted out and they were free to leave. Elizabeth walked stiffly beside James as he led the way back to the sheltered spot where he'd parked the car, gasping as he suddenly stopped and turned her into his arms.

'I can't take much more of this, Beth!' he groaned, as he drew her to him and bent to kiss her. His mouth was hungry for hers and he made no attempt to disguise how he felt, but beneath the passion and the urgency there was still tenderness.

Elizabeth felt her senses explode. She knew James wanted this kiss so much—as she did—yet his hunger was tempered by gentleness, by caring—by everything that made him the man he was. Her heart seemed to open as she realised it.

She kissed him back without reservation, without any attempt to hide how she felt, and she heard him groan again as he drew back. Resting his forehead against hers, he gave a rueful laugh. 'If you had any idea what kissing you does to me...!'

She laughed softly, delighting in the admission, shocked by the fact. She couldn't recall ever feeling this way before—aching for the feel of a man's mouth, yearning for his touch, needing so much more that she could barely contain the urge to draw his head down and kiss him again...and again...

'Mmm, that amuses you, does it? I think a punishment is called for.'

His mouth became even more urgent, more demanding, yet Elizabeth met its demand with an eagerness which simply increased their mutual hunger. When his lips parted so that he could deepen the kiss she responded immediately, shuddering as she felt the warm sweep of his tongue against hers. Beneath her palms his heart was pounding, echoing the heavy beat of hers.

When he drew back this time there was both triumph and uncertainty in his blue eyes as they lingered on her flushed face, a vulnerability and need which made her ache as she saw it.

'Are you sure you don't know why you've been acting so strangely around me, Beth?'

He didn't add anything more as he unlocked the car door for her. Elizabeth got in, faintly stunned by what had happened and its swift ending. She watched the road being swallowed up as they drove back to Yewdale, her mind and body in turmoil as she thought about the question. Why had she treated James so badly?

He drew up in front of her house and turned to her, his eyes playing over her face as though he sensed her confusion. 'Sometimes you have to look deep into yourself to find the answers, Beth. It isn't easy but it's the only way to discover the truth.'

He bent and brushed her mouth with another exquisitely light kiss, then pushed back a wayward curl from her cheek with a gentle hand. 'I'll speak to you soon.'

'Won't you come in for coffee?' she offered shakily, not wanting him to leave. What did he mean about looking for the truth? The question both scared and excited her because she wasn't sure what she might find if she looked too hard.

'Not now. I promised Annie that I'd call in and tell them how Chloe was, and they'll be waiting for me.' He cupped her cheek, his eyes holding hers fast. 'And I think you need a little time to yourself to think things through. Don't rush. There'll be all the time in the world for coffee...and everything else.'

He gave a gently knowing laugh as he leaned across to open the door for her. Elizabeth took a deep breath as he drove away but it did nothing to quieten her thundering heart. Maybe there wasn't any rush but surely it was time she did as he'd said and looked at her feelings...

She let herself in, knowing she was putting off the moment because she was still afraid. Some time soon she had to grasp her courage with both hands...

'What are you doing on Friday night, Liz?'

Elizabeth looked up as Abbie came into the room. It was Tuesday lunchtime and surgery had just finished. She had a couple of calls to do but was writing up some notes before going out. 'Friday? Nothing, as far as I recall. Why?'

'Because it's my birthday and I've decided to have a party!' Abbie grinned as she came and perched on the edge of the desk. 'Sam has been on and on at me about doing something to mark the occasion so I finally gave in!'

'Is...is James going?' Elizabeth flushed, wishing she hadn't asked that when she saw the speculative look Abbie gave her. In the past two days she and James had talked on several occasions, discussing work and various problems, but not once had he mentioned Saturday or what had been said then, and Elizabeth wasn't sure if she was vexed or pleased about that.

Surely, if it mattered to him, James should be curious to know if she'd done as he'd suggested and looked for answers as to why she'd treated him so oddly? But if he

was at all interested he'd managed to hide it very well
so far!

'Of course James is coming. Is that a problem, Liz?'
Abbie asked softly.

'Of course not! Why should you imagine it is?'
Elizabeth struggled to keep her tone light but she knew
she'd failed when she saw the other woman's brows rise.

'Oh, I could make a list as long as my arm, that's
why. Face it, Liz, you've been acting very strangely
around James ever since he got here.' Abbie grinned
wickedly. 'If I didn't know better I might think you had
a thing about him!'

'Of course not!' Elizabeth got up and went to the window, unable to sit a moment longer under Abbie's knowing scrutiny.

'Oh, come on, Liz, this is *me* you're talking to! I know
you. I've seen how you've been behaving lately and it
doesn't take much to put two and two together.' Abbie's
tone softened. 'Why do you imagine you've been so
antagonistic towards James since he arrived? All I can
say is that James is a nice guy. If you're attracted to him
don't make the mistake of doing nothing about it because it seems safer.'

'Safer... James said that too, about not being afraid
to take risks...' Elizabeth was talking more to herself
than Abbie. She flushed as she heard Abbie laugh sympathetically.

'And he was right. Be brave, Liz. Stop trying to be
sensible because, believe me, it doesn't work.' Abbie
grimaced. 'And here endeth the first lesson! Sorry to
preach but I wouldn't do it if I didn't want you to be
happy.'

Abbie gave her a last encouraging smile before she
left the room. Elizabeth stared out of the window, her
mind racing. She'd thought that quietly loving David

was all she'd wanted from life but now she was no longer sure that it was enough. Surely she wanted more than a pleasant, safe relationship based on friendship? Didn't she deserve more?

She closed her eyes, trying to imagine a relationship with David based on desire, but it was impossible. She simply didn't feel that way about him! She couldn't imagine *ever* feeling for David what she'd felt in James's arms—all that hunger and need, that urgency to give him every scrap of herself and take every tiny bit of him for her own...

She took a deep breath as the thought blossomed. She couldn't imagine feeling that way about any man, apart from James! Suddenly it was all shockingly, wonderfully, clear.

She loved David as a friend and colleague but she wasn't in love with him. That honour went to James— James who'd turned her life upside down, James who'd brought her to life. She must have sensed how easy it would be to fall in love with him from the first time she'd seen him and that was why she'd been so on edge around him, so confused. She'd looked at James and had seen danger lurking in his beautiful blue eyes, and had heeded the warning.

It was all so simple yet so complex. She might be in love with him but how did he feel about her? Were a few—admittedly passionate—kisses a true indication of his feelings?

Elizabeth closed her eyes as another thought struck her like a dash of cold water. And how did James feel about Harriet? He'd said that their relationship was over but that didn't mean he was no longer in love with the other woman, did it?

Elizabeth's heart ached. Who did James love? It was

such a simple question but it had the power to change her whole life.

Elizabeth was glad that she was kept busy that afternoon as it gave her little further time to brood. Realising that she was in love with James both scared her and filled her with a sense of elation. It seemed that being in love was just as confusing as any other state of mind!

Surprisingly, few people turned up for surgery that night so that she got through her list in record time. She was about to have a word with Eileen after her last patient left when she almost ran right into James as he came out of his room at the same moment.

'Oops, we do keep on bumping into one another, don't we, Beth?'

The warmly intimate note in his voice made a shudder run down her spine. Elizabeth tried to keep her emotions in check but it was so difficult now she understood how she felt. She loved James! She wanted to shout it from the rooftops, write it in ten-foot-high letters, tell everyone the truth—

'Beth?' There was a hint of uncertainty in his voice that brought her eyes winging to his face. Elizabeth made no attempt to hide what she was feeling and she saw a muscle start to beat in his jaw as he reached out—

'You two finished as well? Quiet night for once, wasn't it?' David came out of his room, smiling as he saw them in the corridor. 'I must say I'm glad of an early finish. It's parents' night tonight at Mike's school so I'd better get over there. See you both tomorrow.'

He gave them a wave before he hurried off. James sighed ruefully. 'This corridor isn't the best place to talk, is it?'

'No, Sam will be finishing in a minute, I expect.' She

took a quick breath, her heart bumping away. 'Do...do you fancy coming round for something to eat again to-night?' she offered huskily. It was the sweetest torment imaginable to stand there, feeling all that she did for him, and not be able to tell him that!

A smile curved his mobile mouth. 'I'd like that, Beth. I'd like that very much indeed. What time do you want me?'

Now! she wanted to cry—here, now, this very sec-cnd—but of course, she didn't say any such thing. 'Around seven?' she suggested as coolly as she could, only it wasn't that cool an answer from the way his eyes suddenly blazed.

He bent and kissed her, just once, so quickly that she barely had chance to register what was happening. 'Seven it is.'

Elizabeth watched him leave, wondering if her heart was going to beat itself right out of her chest. There had been something about the way James had looked at her just now which had wiped away any fears she'd had. There seemed to be wings on her feet as she hurried into the house and informed Mrs Lewis that Dr Sinclair was coming to dinner.

Leaving the housekeeper happily fussing over whether there were enough vegetables prepared, she ran upstairs to shower then tried to decide what to wear. She took a dress from the wardrobe and held it in front of her as she looked in the mirror. She saw the excitement in her eyes and the colour that touched her cheeks and felt joy envelop her from head to toe. She wanted to look her very best tonight when she told James that she loved him—

The bell rang suddenly and Elizabeth frowned. Laying the dress on the bed, she went to the door and listened to the murmur of voices from downstairs. One was obviously Mrs Lewis but the other female voice wasn't one she recognised.

Slipping her skirt and blouse back on, she hurried downstairs, unable to explain the sense of foreboding she felt as she saw the elegant brunette standing in the hall. The woman glanced around as she heard Elizabeth's footsteps and her eyes were hard before she fixed a polished smile to her lips.

'You must be Dr Allen. I'm so sorry to disturb you at this time of night, but I was wondering if you could tell me where James is?' She gave a tinkly laugh as Mrs Lewis excused herself. 'I'm afraid your housekeeper was rather reluctant to tell me, although I can't imagine why!'

'Surgery has just finished so I imagine that Mrs Lewis was trying to stop James from being disturbed.' Elizabeth struggled to keep a rein on her emotions but it wasn't easy. Who was this woman? And why did she have this horrible feeling of dread? 'He isn't on call tonight but I can arrange for you to see the doctor on duty if you have a problem.'

'Oh, I'm not a patient. Heavens, I hope I don't look as though I need to see James in any professional capacity!' Once again she gave that laugh, which grated, the amusement in her green eyes not quite disguising their hardness. 'My reason for seeing James is purely personal, I assure you. I'm Harriet Carr, James's fiancée. You may have heard of me.'

Elizabeth felt a wave of nausea rise into her throat but somehow managed to swallow it. 'Yes, I've heard of you, Miss Carr.'

'You have? Good! It makes things so much easier, doesn't it? Saves all those boring explanations about what I'm doing here!' Harriet replied with a confident smile.

Elizabeth bit her lip to hold back a cry of pain. She looked at the woman standing in the hall and it was as though she were watching all her dreams being crushed. What a fool she'd been to dream them in the first place! But Harriet was right because there was no need for explanations. James's fiancée…that said it all!

CHAPTER ELEVEN

Two things happened then at almost the same moment. The doorbell rang and the old grandfather clock chimed the hour. Seven o'clock.

Elizabeth took a deep breath, praying that Harriet couldn't tell how she was feeling from her tone. 'That should be James now, I imagine. He...he was calling round this evening. I'll let him in.'

'Don't tell him I'm here!' Harriet laughed girlishly, which was quite at odds with the sophisticated picture she presented. She gave Elizabeth another of those cold-eyed smiles. 'I want to surprise him, you see. That's why I didn't phone ahead to let him know I was coming.'

'Of course.' Elizabeth felt as though her smile was glued into place. Her face was aching from the sheer effort of keeping up the front. She went to the door and mentally steeled herself as she opened it.

'Hello, Beth.' James gave her a warm smile. His eyes were full of tenderness and something which made her heart race for a foolish moment before she got herself under control. Whatever she was looking for didn't exist, at least not for her! It was the woman standing across the hall who had the right to that—James's fiancée.

'Beth?' He sounded puzzled as she stood there, without speaking. When he reached out to touch her she quickly evaded him.

'Come in, James. You timed your arrival perfectly.'

'I'm sorry. I don't know—'

'Hello, darling.' Harriet's tone was husky as she came forward to greet him. Elizabeth stepped aside, deliber-

155

ately turning to close the door so that she wouldn't have
to see his expression. How did he feel, seeing Harriet
again? she wondered sickly. Pleased? Delighted?
Thrilled that the woman he loved had come after him at
last?

Her hands shook as she pushed the lock into place. It
took every scrap of composure she could muster to turn.
She felt the floor tilt beneath her as she took in the scene.
Harriet's arms were locked around James's neck as she
raised her face for his kiss...

'Excuse me.' Elizabeth hurried past them, taking ref-
uge in the sitting-room and closing the door so that she
wouldn't have to be privy to any loving confidences. She
didn't need to see or hear what was happening to know
what was going on!

She wasn't sure how long she stood there in the middle of the room, her mind and body numb with the pain
of what had happened. It might have been a minute or
it might have been hours before the door suddenly
opened and James appeared. He gave her a long, steady
look but it was impossible to tell what he was thinking.

'I had no idea that Harriet was coming,' he said quietly, his tone giving little away.

'So I gathered. It...it must have been a surprise for
you.' Her voice shook a little and she bit her lip as she
walked over to the window. All she had left was her
pride and she clung to it desperately, unable to bear the
thought of him knowing how hurt she was.

'It was—a big surprise. I never thought—' He stopped
abruptly, glancing towards the hall. 'Maybe this isn't the
best time to discuss it, Elizabeth.'

So she was Elizabeth again, she thought bitterly. What
had happened to Beth, that tender little diminutive? Or
didn't he need to be tender towards her now that the
woman he really loved had come back to him?

Tears stung her eyes at that thought and she kept her face averted in case he saw them. She heard him give a heavy sigh tinged with impatience.

'Look, please try to understand that I never expec—'

He broke off as the door opened and Harriet came into the room. She gave a little moue of displeasure as she glanced from James's set face to Elizabeth's averted one.

'Oh, dear, I hope I'm not interrupting anything. You both look rather grim.'

'Of course not,' James turned to her with a smile that gave little away. 'We were just discussing a problem we have.'

'Oh, not work again! Darling, don't you ever think of anything else?' Harriet slipped her arm through his and nestled her head on his shoulder. 'Seems to me you need taking out of yourself—and I'm just the person to do it!' She gave Elizabeth a faintly mocking look. 'I'm sure you're exactly the same, Dr Allen, so wrapped up in your work that it takes over everything you do. I hope you have someone to make you see that there's more to life than medicine—as James has me!'

Elizabeth struggled to find something to say but words were beyond her at that moment. She saw James cast her a worried glance and knew that she couldn't take any more of this…this charade! She didn't want his pity or his guilt at having led her to believe something which could never come true. She just wanted him to leave while she still had her dignity intact.

Maybe he sensed how she was feeling because he suddenly turned towards the door. 'I think it's time Harriet and I left. Tell Mrs Lewis I'm sorry if she's gone to any trouble, will you, Elizabeth?'

'Don't worry about it,' Elizabeth followed them from the room. Her legs felt like two pieces of rubber so that every step threatened to be her last. It was only the thought of the commotion it would cause if she collapsed that kept her upright.

'Lovely to meet you, Dr Allen.' Harriet offered a beautifully manicured hand and Elizabeth shook it obediently.

She let it go as soon as good manners permitted, pinning a smile to her stiff mouth again. 'And you, Miss Carr.'

'Oh, make that Harriet...please!' Harriet cast a confident glance at James. 'I'm determined to start as I mean to go on, by making friends with all James's new colleagues. It will make life so much more pleasant to know that I have friends here in the town.'

More pleasant when she moved here to live? Was that what she was saying? Elizabeth couldn't bear to imagine how she was going to feel if that happened! She opened the door abruptly, unable to keep up the pretence of politeness a moment longer.

'I'll speak to you in the morning, Elizabeth.' James lingered as Harriet climbed into the expensive sports car that was parked in the drive.

'Of course. I'll see you in the surgery, I expect.' Her tone was cool, the faint tremor she heard in it hopefully not obvious to him.

His face darkened, his blue eyes filling with a sudden fire as he bent towards her. 'Look, Beth, I know what you're thinking but—'

'Do you?' Her anger rose, fed by all the pain she felt. 'Then you must know that I don't want to discuss this any further!' She looked pointedly towards the car. 'Your fiancée is waiting, James.'

He uttered what might have been a curse before he strode down the steps and got into the car. Elizabeth shut the door immediately. She didn't need to watch him drive off into the sunset with another woman to know that there was nothing between them!

It was barely eight when Elizabeth went through to the surgery the following morning. She couldn't face staying in the house any longer, going over and over what had happened the night before. She hadn't slept at all, just lain awake as that scene had replayed endlessly inside her head. Harriet's arms around James's neck as she'd raised her face for his kiss...

Her eyes blurred with tears as she pushed open the door so it was a moment before she spotted the man standing by the window with his back to her. Her heart began to pound as he turned slowly and she saw the strain etched on his handsome face. It looked as though James, too, had spent a sleepless night but she didn't want to think of the reason. The thought that James had spent the night with Harriet, making up for the weeks they had been apart, was too much to bear!

'Hello, Beth. I wanted to catch you while there was nobody about.'

Her hands shook as he called her by that special name. She turned to close the door, using the few seconds to get a grip on herself, but she knew he'd seen how upset she was. He came towards her and his eyes seemed to blaze as he took in her white face.

'You have to listen to me! I had no idea that Harriet was going to turn up like that yesterday,' he grated. He reached for her hand but Elizabeth snatched it away.

'So you said last night. Look, James, I really can't see any point in this. What happens between you and Harriet is your business,' she said flatly.

'I see. So you're not interested in listening to what I have to say?' He drew back abruptly, his face settling into such grim lines that she shivered. He looked so distant all of a sudden that her heart ached even more.

'No. Frankly, I...I cannot see any point, can you?' Her voice caught and she had to clear her throat before she could continue. 'Obviously, your main concern now is sorting things out with Harriet. Please don't feel that you have to explain anything because I...I understand.'

'Do you?' James gave a deep laugh. There was an edge to it which made her pulse leap but Elizabeth refused to let him see how it affected her.

She went and sat down at her desk, taking a letter from the tray and staring at it while she tried to collect herself. She wouldn't break down! She wouldn't embarrass either of them, by doing that.

'Are you sure you understand the situation properly, Elizabeth?'

His tone was openly sceptical and she looked up, puzzled by the intensity of the look he gave her. Her answer was obviously important to him but why?

The reason slid into her mind and she had to bite her lip to hold back a burst of hysterical laughter. Was James worried that she might say something to Harriet and spoil things for him?

'Yes, I understand, James—perfectly.' It was hard to control the pain, which felt as if it were ripping her heart to shreds, but she struggled on. 'I have no intention of...of saying anything to Harriet if that's what you're worried about.'

'Worried...?' He frowned heavily so that Elizabeth felt a momentary qualm, but she had to sort this out here and now.

'About us and...and what happened the other day.' She lowered her gaze, staring down at the letter until the words blurred. 'It was just a brief interlude, nothing more. And I'm sure that Harriet wouldn't blame you in the circumstances. After all, you had no idea that she was going to come back into your life at that point, had you?'

'No. I can honestly say that I never expected this to happen.' There was a tinge of dryness in his voice which made her look up. Elizabeth felt her heart judder as she saw the tender light in his eyes, then it struck her that he must be thinking about his fiancée.

Tears blurred her vision and she looked down at the letter again before he saw them. 'I only hope that things work out the way you want them to, James,' she said huskily.

'Oh, they will. You can be sure of that.' He gave a confident laugh as he strode to the door. 'I don't intend to let anything go wrong this time because I'm taking no chances whatsoever with the future!'

Elizabeth waited until the door had closed behind him before she gave in to her grief. It was too poignant to think about the future James was planning and know that she would never be part of it.

Over the next two days Elizabeth went out of her way to avoid running into James. She knew from the rumours that were flying around town that Harriet Carr was staying at the Fleece, and put her own interpretation on what that meant.

So what if they were staying there together, possibly even sharing a room? It wasn't any of her business.

'Real hoity-toity madam she is, too! You should have heard her telling Rose that the bathroom might be clean by Rose's standards but not by hers.' Peg Ryan, who cleaned both at the surgery and the pub, sounded well and truly put out. 'I said to Rose I bin doin' this job for twenty years and there's never bin a complaint before!

How that nice Dr Sinclair got mixed up with someone like that I don't know!'

Elizabeth looked up from the report she was reading as the conversation came floating through the half-open door. It was still early and so far only Peg and Eileen had arrived for work that day. That she derived a crumb of comfort from what she'd overheard wasn't to her credit. It seemed that Harriet wasn't making a very good impression!

'I know, Peg. Rose told me that she's been no end of trouble, asking for all sorts of special things to eat and turning up her nose at the menu,' Eileen answered. 'Rose said she won't be sorry to see the back of her.'

'Me neither!' Peg unplugged the vacuum cleaner with a vicious hand. 'She was real nasty to my Benny yesterday. He only wanted to show Dr Sinclair this new kitten he's got but that madam told him to go away and stop pestering. She had the nerve to ask Rose why Benny wasn't in a home as it was obvious it wasn't safe for him to be left running round town by himself!'

Elizabeth gasped in dismay. Surely Harriet hadn't been so unfeeling? Admittedly, Peg's twenty-year-old son had learning disabilities but he wasn't a danger to anyone. Benny had the mind of an eight-year-old child inside the body of a grown man, a Peter Pan figure whom the whole town looked out for. Harriet wasn't doing herself any favours, by saying such things. She would simply end up alienating herself from the towns-folk, making it difficult when she moved here to live.

Was that her intention? Elizabeth wondered suddenly. Harriet had implied that she intended to join James in Yewdale, but maybe she'd changed her mind now that she'd realised how keen he was to fall in with her wishes? Perhaps she'd insisted that he move back to

London, in which case it would make little difference
what impression she made on the people of Yewdale.

Elizabeth stared down at the journal in front of her
but it was impossible to concentrate. She wasn't sure
which was the most painful—the thought of seeing
James and Harriet together if they lived in Yewdale or
never seeing James at all if he moved back to London.
Whatever he decided, though, would have nothing to do
with her, and that was the most painful thought of all.

'You haven't forgotten about my party tonight, Liz?'
Abbie stuck her head round the surgery door on Friday
morning.

'No, of course not.' Elizabeth managed a smile. 'Only
I offered to swop with Sam as he was due to be on call
tonight.'

'I hope he didn't come up with some sob story to
persuade you?' Abbie grimaced. 'That man could make
a saint feel guilty. His powers of persuasion should be
bottled. A dose of the O'Neill charm and people would
be queuing up to do you favours!'

'Sounds like a back-handed compliment to me!'
Elizabeth laughed, trying to keep up the pretence that
everything was normal—as she'd tried so hard to do all
week. 'Anyway, Sam didn't persuade me. I offered.'

'But you're still coming, aren't you?' Abbie shot a
glance over her shoulder then came into the room and
closed the door. 'Look, Liz, it isn't any of my business
but I know how upset you've been. Not that I blame
you. Having that woman turn up out of the blue must
have been a blow. But take my word for it that all the
stories flying around town are so much hot air. James is
never going to be fool enough to take up with her again!'

'I think that's his business. It has nothing to do with
anyone—'

'Liz! This is me you're talking to—Aunty Abbie, founder member of the broken hearts club! I know what you're going through, believe me. I've been there, done that and worn the T-shirt! Have some guts, girl. If you love the man fight for him. Don't let that whey-faced woman ruin your life!'

Abbie strode to the door. She cast a glance over her shoulder. 'Be there tonight, Liz. And in your best dress. Let him see what he's in danger of losing.'

She was gone in a whirl. Elizabeth stared at the door with a rueful smile. Put like that it sounded so simple, but it wasn't. You couldn't make someone love you. She couldn't *make* James love her! If it was Harriet he wanted then she had to accept that. But she'd go to the party tonight, go there and make herself see the situation for what it was. She'd spent too many years pretending to start doing it again.

It was painful to face it but maybe it was better to have known what love was, even for such a short time, than to have lived her life accepting second-best. She might regret the fact that James didn't love her but she would never, ever, regret loving him!

Elizabeth stopped in front of the mirror and studied her reflection. She had chosen to wear the jade green dress again that night, with the same brooch pinned to her shoulder and the same delicate earrings swaying gently from her ears. She was even wearing the high-heeled black sandals, her legs looking long and shapely with the added height. It was strange to wear the outfit and recall how different she'd felt just a few short weeks ago when she'd worn it last. She'd been beset by uncertainties then, unable to understand her reaction to James...

She sighed as she picked up her bag. There was no point in going back over what had happened. She had to look forward—to this night and to all the other nights to come. Maybe she should think about leaving Yewdale and going further afield, looking for something which would offer her the fulfilment she needed.

But without James would she ever achieve that? a small voice inside whispered. How could her life ever be truly complete without him as a part of it?

Determinedly, she closed her mind to that thought as she ran downstairs. Mrs Lewis was just crossing the hall and she stopped when she saw her. 'Oh, you do look nice, Miss Elizabeth. That dress suits you a treat, it does.'

'Thank you, Mrs Lewis. To be honest, I wasn't sure if I could be bothered going tonight. I'm on call, you see.'

'Oh, be silly to miss out. You might not get any calls, with a bit of luck.' Mrs Lewis gave her a guileless smile. 'I expect everyone will be there—Dr Sinclair as well, I imagine. I'm glad he got rid of that woman. Good riddance to her is all I can say!'

'I'm sorry, I don't understand.' Elizabeth felt her heart give one huge surge as though it were going to leap right out of her chest, given the chance. 'Has...has Miss Carr left?'

'Just after lunch today. Rose said that she paid her bill then upped and left before they knew what was happening.' Mrs Lewis sounded smug. 'I expect Dr Sinclair will tell you all about it when you see him tonight.'

'I...I expect so,' Elizabeth had to swallow to ease the lump in her throat. What did it mean? Had Harriet left so suddenly because James had asked her to? Or was it simply that now everything was settled between them there was no need for her to stay any longer? Maybe Harriet had returned to London to start putting their plans into action—finding another flat where they could live, making all the dozens of arrangements necessary to reorganize their lives...

Elizabeth felt she'd go mad if she didn't find out the truth. She picked up her jacket, hearing the house-keeper's cluck of concern. 'Are you sure you're feeling all right, Miss Elizabeth? You've gone quite pale—'

'I'm fine.' Elizabeth cut short the show of concern, not wanting anything to delay her. She would speak to James, find out what had happened. And then what? That was the sixty-four-thousand-dollar question! What was she going to do?

Her mind was in turmoil as she left the house and drove into town, her thoughts jumping ahead to when she would see James. Should she speak to him first? Or would he speak to her...?

She nearly jumped out of her skin as her mobile phone rang. Pulling into the kerb, she answered it quickly. 'Dr Allen.'

'Oh, Dr Allen, I don't know what to do! It all got out of hand, you see. Barry didn't mean half the things he said...'

There was a noisy sobbing at the other end of the line. Elizabeth frowned as she tried to piece together what she'd heard. 'Barry? Barry Jackson, do you mean?'

'Yes! It's me, Annie. I should have said.' The woman broke into loud sobs again and Elizabeth sighed.

'Look, Annie, you're going to have to calm down and tell me what's wrong.' An awful thought struck her. 'Nothing has happened to Chloe, has it?'

'Course not! Dr Mackenzie phoned this afternoon to say that our Darren is a good match for when they need to do that bone-marrow transplant. He's really thrilled about it, too.'

Annie took a deep breath. 'It's our Sophie, you see. She told us tonight about the baby and everything. Barry went mad, said he was going to break his neck if he got his hands on him, and Sophie went running out of the house. Now I don't know what to do because I can't find her anywhere!'

'Break whose neck? Do you mean the father of Sophie's baby?' It was like patching together a jigsaw-puzzle but Elizabeth forced herself to be patient, not that it was easy.

'Yes, young Billy Murray—that's who it is. I expect Sophie's gone there to warn him her dad's out for blood, but she were that upset. Anything could happen to her, Dr Allen. Anything at all!'

Elizabeth sighed as she glanced at her watch. 'I don't suppose it's worth me telling you to call the police and have them go over to the farm?' She carried on when there was silence at the other end of the line. 'No, I didn't think so. Look, Annie, I really don't know what I can do…'

'Can you go and see if you can find her, Dr Allen? Have a talk to her, like. Please! We've no car, as you know, and she were that upset. I'm frightened she might, well, she might do something silly!'

'Surely not. Sophie seems like a sensible enough girl—' Elizabeth began, then cut off the rest of the sentence. It was hardly the most appropriate description in the circumstances! 'All right, Annie, I'll drive over to the Murrays' place and see if she's there. If she isn't, though, you're going to have to phone the police whether you like it or not.'

She cut the connection and wasted no time in turning the car to head out to Boundary Farm, where Billy lived with his parents and his grandfather, Fred. It was at least a twenty-minute drive, but in all conscience she couldn't leave Sophie, wandering around on a night like this, if she could do something about it. A thin mist had started to fall, settling over the countryside and leaving a damp veil on the grass and trees.

Elizabeth switched on her headlights as she left the town behind, reducing her speed as the mist got thicker. It was difficult to see where she was going, but she knew the roads so well that it helped—

She bit off a shocked exclamation as something appeared directly in the centre of the road ahead of her. She slammed on the brakes, slewed to a halt and took a shaky breath to steady her nerves. She opened the car door to be greeted by the excited barking of the dog she'd almost run over. The Border collie came bounding over to her, almost frantic with excitement as she bent to pat it.

'Good girl,' Elizabeth said soothingly, stroking its silky head. She frowned as she suddenly realised it was Isaac Shepherd's dog. 'Hello, Tess. What are you doing out here?'

The dog gave a little yelp as she recognised her name then suddenly turned and ran a little way back down the road. She stopped beside the stone wall, whining pitifully. Elizabeth went to her, wondering what the matter was with the dog and why it was roaming about on such a night.

Tess whined again then suddenly jumped over the wall and stood beside the path which led up onto the hills, her tongue lolling out and her intelligent eyes pleading.

'Do you want me to follow you, Tess? Is that it?'

The dog gave another little bark, almost as though she'd understood. She ran up the path a short way then came back again and waited expectantly. Elizabeth peered towards the dark slopes of the hill, but she could see nothing from where she stood. Had there been an accident? Was that what Tess was telling her? Maybe

Isaac had had a fall and the dog was trying to lead her to him.

Elizabeth didn't waste any more time. She ran back to her car, groaning as she tried to ring for help and found the phone dead. There were pockets in the area where it was impossible to catch a signal, making the phone useless, and this was one of them.

Reaching into the glove compartment, Elizabeth hunted out the heavy-duty torch she always carried and checked the battery, before going back to where the dog was still patiently waiting for her. 'OK, Tess, lead on. But if this is a wild-goose chase I warn you I won't be pleased!'

Tess gave one great excited bark and raced off into the mist. Elizabeth took a last look at the road and sighed as she turned to follow the dog up the hill. Of all the times for this to happen. Somebody up there must be playing tricks on her!

CHAPTER TWELVE

'HERE, Tess, wait! Good girl...'

Elizabeth paused to catch her breath as the collie stopped obediently. The mist had thickened so that she could see barely five yards in front of her now. Night was drawing in as well, making it doubly difficult to tell where she was, but she'd tried to keep track as the dog had led her up the hillside. By her reckoning, Isaac Shepherd's house should be below to her left and the road to her right. It made her feel a bit easier to have some idea which way to go in order to fetch help.

Spurred on by that thought, she set off again, wishing she'd thought to change out of the sandals before following the dog. It was difficult to keep her footing on the scree-covered escarpment over which Tess was leading her. She made it to the other side and quickened her pace, urged on by the dog's mounting excitement as it raced on ahead. Elizabeth felt a wave of relief as she caught sight of a figure, lying on the ground in the lee of a large boulder.

She ran forward, pushing Tess out of the way as she knelt down. 'Isaac...Can you hear me? It's Dr Allen.'

'Aye, I can hear you. I might be an old fool but I'm not a deaf one!' Isaac rasped hoarsely. He lifted a gnarled hand and patted the collie's head as she lay beside him. 'So you found someone, did you, Tess? Good lass.'

Tess gave a whimper of pleasure at the praise. She inched forward until she was lying pressed against his side. Elizabeth let her be as she bent to examine Isaac.

He was very cold and the warmth from the dog's body would help stave off hypothermia, always a risk when something like this happened.

'What happened, Isaac?' she asked as she checked his pulse, frowning as she felt how erratic it was. 'Did you fall or what?'

'This damned heart of mine, that's what did it!' he replied gruffly. 'I had this pain, see, right down my arm and across my chest...' He sighed, his face looking gaunt and grey in the torchlight. 'I must have passed out because when I came round it was growing dusk. I tried to get up but I couldn't manage more than a step or two. That's why I lay down again and sent Tess off for help.'

'I see.' Elizabeth managed a smile, though the situation didn't sound too good. From what Isaac had said, and what she could tell, he seemed to have suffered a heart attack. 'Well, Tess did her job really well. She sat in the middle of the road so that I had to stop, didn't you, girl?'

'She's a good lass, right enough.' Isaac gasped as another spasm hit him. Elizabeth waited until it had passed, wondering what she was going to do. He needed medical attention urgently and yet there was little hope of her being able to get him down off the hill by herself.

'I think I need to go for help, Isaac,' she explained quietly. 'I don't like leaving you but there's no way I can get you down from here all by myself.'

'I understand. It's nobbut me own fault, silly old fool as I am.' Isaac grimaced. 'Frank's been on and on at me but I wouldn't listen.'

'Well, worry about that later,' Elizabeth said as she stood up. 'I think the farm is in that direction—am I right?'

'Aye, but it's not the easiest walk, lass.' Isaac

frowned. 'I don't want you putting yourself in danger for my sake.'

'I'll take it steady, I promise you. Now, what I want you to—' She broke off as Tess jumped up suddenly and began to bark loudly. Elizabeth peered through the gloom and gasped as a figure loomed into sight. For a moment she thought she must be dreaming and then James was beside her, reaching out to draw her into his arms and hold her close.

'Are you OK, Beth?' Even as he asked the question his hands were running over her, as though he needed to check for himself that she wasn't hurt. Elizabeth took a shaky breath but it wasn't nearly enough to rid herself of the dizzy incredulity she felt. What was James doing here?

'Mrs Lewis called me. Annie Jackson rang the house to say that she kept trying your phone and couldn't get an answer,' he explained, as though she'd asked the question out loud.

'She wanted me to look for Sophie. There'd been a row and she was worried that the girl might do something silly. I was on my way over to the Murrays' place to see if she was there when I saw Tess sitting in the middle of the road.'

'Tess?' James frowned, then laughed softly. 'The dog. And she led you up here? So that's why I found your car abandoned in the middle of nowhere like that. I had the fright of my life, finding it there with you gone.'

His voice grated and Elizabeth smiled gently. 'I'm sorry. I did try to phone for help but the mobile wouldn't work. It never crossed my mind that anyone would come looking for me, although how you found me in this mist I've no idea.'

'Sheer desperation, I'd call it.' He took a deep breath,

before letting her go and glancing at Isaac. 'So, what have we got, Beth?'

It was the 'we' that did it, that one small word. Elizabeth felt a huge wave of relief run through her as she knew suddenly that everything was going to be all right. Her voice was filled with happiness, so out of keeping with the actual words. 'Myocardial infarction, from the look of it.'

James's eyes were full of something which made her feel as though she would burst with joy as he looked at her. 'Then I think we'd better see about getting Mr Shepherd down off this hill as fast as possible.' He smiled at the old man. 'The best place for you is hospital, I think.'

Isaac grunted. 'Never thought I'd see the day when I agreed to that, but I think you're right, doctor.'

It was James who made the descent to the farm to ring for an ambulance and the mountain rescue team, who'd be needed to carry Isaac Shepherd down the hill. He refused Elizabeth's offer to go, pointing out that he'd be able to make the journey far faster than she could hope to.

Elizabeth tried to argue the point but James refused to be budged once he'd made up his mind. 'No way am I allowing you to go wandering around these hills in this mist!' He led her a little away from the man on the ground. Taking her face between his hands, he kissed her quickly. 'I couldn't bear the thought of anything happening to you, my darling.'

Elizabeth wet her lips with the very tip of her tongue. 'But Harriet…?'

'Gone…for good!' He gave her another quick kiss then was gone himself, leaving her seething with questions. Did that mean what it seemed to—that his relationship with Harriet was really and truly over?

The ensuing wait seemed agonisingly long. Elizabeth fought to keep a grip on her composure as she tended to Isaac, keeping him warm with her own jacket and talking to him to keep his spirits up, but at the back of her mind the questions hummed away insistently. Had James meant what he'd said? And, if he had, what did it mean for her?

By the time she heard voices, coming up the hill, Elizabeth was almost at the end of her tether. She got to her feet stiffly as a small party appeared, and smiled in relief as she saw James at the end of it.

'Are you all right?' he asked, as soon as he reached her.

'Fine.'

There was no time for anything else as they set about supervising Isaac being loaded onto the stretcher for the journey back down the hill. The mountain rescue people carried oxygen with them as a matter of course, and James fitted the mask over the old man's face to help ease his breathing before they set off.

The ambulance was waiting at the farm and the paramedics soon loaded Isaac on board and roared away. There were other people there as well—Harvey Walsh, who'd heard the sirens and had come to see what was going on, and Sid and Dorothy Fielding, Cathy's parents, who'd been going home after a day out in Kendal. Within a very short time everything had been arranged.

Harvey would take care of the farm until something could be worked out and he'd take Tess home with him in the meantime. Sid and Dorothy Fielding were going to drop in on Frank to let him know what had happened, rather than have him hear the news over the phone.

James shook his head in amazement as they all drove off. 'It just comes naturally to them, doesn't it? They really want to help one of their neighbours when there's trouble.'

'It's that sort of community. Oh, it isn't all peace and harmony by any means. People fall out over trivial little things and don't speak for years on end sometimes, but on the whole people in Yewdale care about each other.' She paused, her nerves so tightly drawn that she was trembling. 'You'll find that out for yourself, if you stay here long enough, James.'

'Something to look forward to. But, then, there's so much else to look forward to, Beth, so much that I've found already since I came here.' He drew her into his arms, lifting her face so that he could look deep into her eyes. 'I love you, Dr Allen. I hope it's something you want to hear me say as much as I want to tell you. I love you with all my heart...despite the fact that you haven't made it easy!'

'Haven't made it...' Elizabeth tried to wriggle free but he held her fast. There were sparks in her hazel eyes as she stared at him. 'And what do you mean by that?'

'Oh, only that you set out to put me off this job and tried your best to persuade me that, first, I wasn't suited to it, second, the job was too much for me to cope with, third—'

'I think I get the picture, James!' Elizabeth replied with a touch of asperity before she gave a rueful sigh. 'I did, though, didn't I? I tried to put you off from the moment you set foot in the town.'

'You did. I think I know why but I'd like to hear you tell me the reason.' His voice was as soft as the wind as he drew her down to sit beside him on the old stone wall. He linked his fingers through hers, lifted her hand to his mouth and kissed her knuckles, smiling as he felt the shiver she gave.

Elizabeth struggled to contain the rush of sensations

she felt at that light caress. She stared off into the distance as she answered his question in a quiet voice. 'I was afraid, James. That's why I behaved the way I did, why I tried to find reasons not to…to like you. I think I must have realised almost from the first time I saw you just how dangerous you were to my peace of mind.'

'Mmm, I must say that I'm delighted to hear it. I had one or two sleepless nights myself before I got here. You had more or less the same effect on me, Beth.' He laughed as she turned to him in surprise.

'I think it was that cool façade you presented. It was such a temptation to find out what was beneath it and whether the warmly passionate woman I suspected really did exist. That's why it came as such an unpleasant shock to discover how you felt about David.'

'Is that why you kept taunting me with it?' she asked, suddenly understanding.

'Yes.' He laughed ruefully as he bent to kiss her with such thoroughness that she almost forgot what she'd asked him. 'The old green-eyed monster rears its head in all sorts of different ways! I could see right away how fond of David you were but gradually—and to my utmost relief, I might add—I began to realise that that was all you felt for him. You weren't in love with him, Beth. You simply thought you were because it was safer.'

Her eyes misted. 'You're right, of course. David was there when I needed someone. I was let down badly in university when my first and only love affair went wrong. I found out that the man I'd believed to be the answer to my dreams was just using me. I was just one of a number of students he'd had affairs with. I came home and poured out the whole miserable tale to David and it made it better in a way.' She gave a little laugh. 'Which should have been an indication that the ill-fated affair hadn't been all that meaningful if I could get over it so quickly!'

'I hope so!' James laughed, but there was a shade of uncertainty in his deep voice.

'I love you, darling! Only you…ever!' Elizabeth kissed him, letting that prove she was telling the truth. She felt him relax, his thumb gently stroking the back of her knuckles in a way which really wasn't conducive to elaborate explanations. She did her best, however, wanting to clear things up. Then she could look ahead to the future… There was a breathy quality to her voice as she wondered what that future might hold.

'After that I latched onto the idea that it was David I loved simply because it was so much safer when there was no possibility of ever being hurt. I've always been the sort of person who hates taking risks and I suppose that played a part in it. That David was quite unaware of how I felt didn't matter at all…which should have shown me sooner that I was fooling myself. It took you to make me take a long, hard look at the situation and see it for what it was, James.'

'And what did you find out then?' There was a need in his voice which made her love him all the more.

'That I love you. That you're the one and only man I need and want in my life from now on. That the only future I have is with you, whether it be here in Yewdale or wherever we decide we want to live.'

'Beth…darling!' His groan was swallowed up as he kissed her with a hungry urgency that made her cling to him. He drew back at last, cupping her cheek with a tender hand. 'I love you so much. It doesn't matter where we live because that won't change, but I'd like it to be here. I might only be a newcomer but I'd like to think of us spending our lives here in this town—and bringing up our children here.'

'Th-that's what I'd like, too.' She smiled up at him, loving every bit of this man who had come into her life and shown her what she really wanted. 'But you are sure—about Harriet and everything?'

'I couldn't be more certain.' His tone was full of assurance, quashing any last doubts she had. 'Harriet and I were finished before I left London. I think it was over a long time ago, to tell the truth, but I didn't do anything about it, which is something I regret. I didn't invite her here. She simply took it into her own head to come.'

He shrugged lightly. 'She used the excuse of there being some business to clear up from the sale of our flat, but I have an idea that it might have been something my mother said which prompted her to come.'

'Your mother? What do you mean?' Elizabeth frowned as she heard him laugh.

'Oh, just that my letters home have been full of you. My mother must have put two and two together and realised what was happening. I suppose she let it slip, either accidentally or deliberately, when Harriet called round to see her. My mother was never that fond of Harriet,' he explained dryly.

'But...but Harriet must still love you if what she heard upset her enough to send her up here.' Elizabeth took a deep breath. It was bitterly painful but she had to be sure he was certain about his feelings. 'Are you sure you won't regret letting Harriet go?'

'I've already told you but I'll tell you again—it's you I love, darling.' He kissed her slowly, letting his lips convince her. He smiled as he saw the expression on her face. 'That's better. As for Harriet being upset, I think the real truth is that she doesn't like to be thwarted. She'd made up her mind that I'd realise I'd made a mistake and was probably waiting for me to contact her.

Hearing that I was not only settling in but was falling desperately in love with another woman wouldn't have pleased her at all!'

'Oh, James, if only I'd listened to you. That was what you were trying to tell me, wasn't it?'

'Yes!' He laughed tenderly, as he kissed the tip of her nose. 'I tried to explain the situation to you but you were so determined not to listen that I decided the best thing to do was to get everything straight first—things like the sale of the flat being finalised, making arrangements to have my furniture shipped up here, all those loose ends.

'Harriet insisted on staying at the Fleece, probably because she hoped it would cause trouble between you and me. However, I made it very clear to her from that first night that I wasn't interested in getting back together with her, and I think the message finally got through. And that, as they say, is that! Now, come here!'

The next ten minutes were deliciously satisfying for both of them. When James finally let her go Elizabeth was dizzy with joy. He helped her down from the wall then bent to look at her passion-drugged eyes with a purely masculine triumph.

'Mmm, that's just what I wanted to see. There's no doubt what you're suffering from.'

Elizabeth laughed huskily. 'And what is that, Doctor?'

'Well, let's run through the symptoms.' He circled her wrist with his fingers. 'Racing pulse for starters.' He placed his hand to her breast, his deeply indrawn breath matching the one she took. His voice was a little rougher as he continued. 'Rapid heartbeat.' He removed his hand with obvious reluctance and tilted her chin. 'Slight fever?'

'So what's your diagnosis?' It was hard to keep the

tremor from her voice and she made no real effort to do so.

'If you want my professional opinion, it looks like a bad case of love to me.'

'And…and is there a cure, Dr Sinclair?'

'No, happily enough, this is one disease that's incurable, although it is possible to do something to alleviate the more distressing symptoms.'

'Indeed? Maybe you should explain that a little better.'

'Oh, there's no maybe about it! It's something I intend to do—soon! Although it might just take a little bit of organising…'

'Organising? What do you mean?' Elizabeth frowned.

'Well, close-knit communities are all well and good but they do tend to make it difficult to enjoy any privacy.' His eyes were full of tenderness as they met hers. 'I want to spend the night with you, Beth. I want to make love to you and go to sleep with you in my arms and wake up with you still there in the morning. However, I can't see Mrs Lewis taking kindly to that idea nor can I see us getting any peace at the Fleece!'

She laughed ruefully. 'I see what you mean. What do you suggest?'

'Oh, I have a plan. Trust me, Beth.'

He didn't say anything more as he led her back along the road to where their cars were parked. Elizabeth got into her car, smiling as James blew her a kiss before they headed back to town. Trusting him now was the easiest thing in the world to do!

Sunlight poured through the window to lie in golden bars across the big double bed. Elizabeth propped herself up on her elbow as she watched James, sleeping. He looked so handsome as he lay there, relaxed and at peace.

She bent and pressed her mouth to his, feeling him come awake immediately. 'Beth...'

There was no hesitation as he said her name. He drew her down to him and kissed her deeply, groaning as he felt her immediate response. It didn't seem to matter that they'd made love until the early hours because she still felt the same desire for him and knew that he felt the same way about her...

There was a knock on the door and she drew the covers up as James dragged on a robe and got up to answer it. He took the breakfast tray from the waiter and carried it over to the table by the window. 'Breakfast, Dr Allen?'

'Mmm, I don't know if I'm hungry—for food,' she teased, stretching luxuriously under the quilt. She gasped as he came back to the bed and scooped her up into his arms, kissing her with such thoroughness that she was dizzy when he finally stopped.

'Think you can tease me, do you?' he growled, nibbling at her neck where a pulse was beating away betrayingly.

Elizabeth put her hands against his chest to push him away as she joined in the seductive little game, and felt her pulse race that bit faster as her fingers encountered warm, bare skin and crisp golden hair. 'I'm a sick woman,' she croaked, knowing that he'd felt her response and had understood its cause. 'You said so last night, James. I have this awful, incurable disease!'

'Lovesickness...terrible.' He sighed as he carried her over to the window and gently deposited her on one of the comfortable chairs. 'You'll need a lot of looking after, Beth. A lot of tender, loving care for starters.'

'Sounds good to me!' She laughed. He bent to pour them both coffee, and she sighed in contentment as she looked out of the window at the view of the lake and thought about what had happened since last night.

Once they'd got back to Yewdale James had left her with strict instructions to pack a bag. He'd ignored her protest that she was on call, telling her that he'd sort everything out—which he had. Sam had rung a short time later, barely able to contain his amusement as he'd informed her that he'd be taking over from her and that she wasn't to worry.

Elizabeth had been flushed even before she'd spoken to Mrs Lewis, but all the housekeeper had done had been to tell her to have a nice time. By the time James had arrived she hadn't known if she was on her head or her heels. They'd driven south to Newby Bridge and had arrived just before night at this hotel, set right on the banks of Lake Windermere. They'd been shown straight to their room and then left alone...

Now as Elizabeth looked at the pale green glitter of the lake she knew that she was happier than she'd ever been.

'Penny for them?'

She turned and smiled as she found James watching her. 'Oh, they're worth far more than that, darling. I was just thinking how happy I am and how much I love you.'

He took her hand, his eyes imbuing the gentle words with everything she could have hoped for. 'And I love you too.'

It was the most glorious, wonderful day Beth could ever remember. They walked by the lake after breakfast then took the ferry to Bowness, sitting on the old-fashioned wooden steamer along with all the tourists.

The sun was setting by the time they got back to the hotel. Elizabeth went to have a shower and change for dinner while James made a few phone calls. They'd decided to stay an extra day so he was ringing David to let him know.

He was smiling as she came back into the room wrapped in a towel. 'Sophie has turned up, you'll be pleased to know. Turns out she hadn't gone to Billy Murray's after all—she was at Trisha Shepherd's, and evidently Barry has calmed down so it looks as though things will work out.'

'Good.' Elizabeth sat down at the dressing-table to dry her hair, smiling at James in the mirror. 'And I suppose you phoned the hospital to find out how Isaac Shepherd is as well?'

He laughed. 'How did you guess? Anyway, he's stable at the moment. Obviously he isn't out of danger but they're hopeful.' He came over and bent to kiss her nape, his lips warm and tender as he nibbled at her skin. 'David said not to worry about what was happening there so I think we'll do just that. Let's forget that we're doctors and concentrate on us!'

They went down to dinner somewhat later than planned. Elizabeth wondered if the happiness she felt was written all over her face as James escorted her to the dining-room. She was just turning to tell him how she felt when someone touched her arm.

'It is you, isn't it? Dr Allen? Remember me?'

Elizabeth frowned as she turned to the young woman who'd accosted her. 'I'm sorry—' she began, then broke off and laughed. 'It's Heather, isn't it? You were the one who had that accident on the motorbike.'

'That's right.' Heather smiled broadly as she drew a

young man forward to join her. 'And this is my husband, Geoff.'

'Well, you look a lot better than you did the last time I saw you.' James shook hands with the younger man. 'Everything all right now?'

'Fine,' Geoff said. 'And it's thanks to you, Dr Sinclair. They told me at the hospital that I might not have survived if you hadn't drained my lung.'

'All part of the job.' James shrugged off the thanks. 'So, what are you doing here?'

'Having our honeymoon—a bit later than planned!' Heather laughed as she linked hands with her husband. 'Our parents clubbed together and paid for a weekend here for us because the other was ruined. But how about you two? Is there a special reason you're here?'

James looked at her and Elizabeth felt her heart thunder as she saw the expression in his eyes. 'Very special. I intend to ask Dr Allen to marry me so wish me luck, won't you both?'

Elizabeth had no idea what the young couple said as James led her away. He cast a glance towards the dining-room then steered her out through the conservatory, which led directly into the garden and from there to the lake. The night was dark now, the air warm and sweet with the scent of the vegetation. Elizabeth drank it all in, wanting to store this moment for ever as she turned to James and found him looking at her with a world of love in his eyes.

'I think I prefer to do this in private, Beth. You never know what the answer's going to be when you ask a question.'

There was the faintest trace of uncertainty in his voice, a hint of vulnerability, which made her love for him blossom. She looked up into his face, smiling gently.

'But sometimes you have to take a risk to get what you really want, James.'

He touched her mouth with the tips of his fingers, his eyes holding hers fast. 'Then will you marry me, Beth—soon?'

She went on tiptoe and pressed her mouth to his, kissing away the uncertainty. 'Yes, oh, yes, James. Very, very soon!'

After that there didn't seem to be much need to say anything else!

EPILOGUE

DAVID ROSS put down the phone after James rang. He smiled to himself as he went into the kitchen and plugged in the kettle. He'd had an idea there'd been something behind the strange way Elizabeth had been behaving lately!

He took a mug from the drainer, promising himself that he'd put the crockery away later. What day was it? Saturday? It was Mike's turn to do the dishes. Though he might wash them, drying was definitely out—especially when he'd made plans to go to the cinema!

David took the cup of coffee through to the sitting-room and sat on the sofa, tossing aside a game Emily had left there. She was at her friend's house and he'd collect her later. The house was quiet without them both, too quiet. It gave him too much time to brood.

He picked up the photo from the table beside him, feeling the sadness he always felt when he thought about Kate. She'd been too young to die—they'd had so much living left to do! The pain had eased now to a dull ache but suddenly he felt angry.

He got up and went to the window. The night was calm but it simply made a mockery of how he felt. He was forty-two years old—his life wasn't over! Suddenly he felt envious of James and Elizabeth, for what they had and what he'd lost...

A light came on in the house next door. David lifted the cup to his lips and drank as he looked at it. He'd seen the 'sold' sticker go up a week or so back but there'd been no sign of anyone moving in. Who'd bought the place? Another family? A couple?

He turned away with a sigh. It wasn't going to make any difference to him who'd be living next door...

*   *   *   *   *

*Look next month
for David's story in*
OUR NEW MUMMY
*The second marvellous instalment
in* A COUNTRY PRACTICE

MILLS & BOON®

Makes any time special

Enjoy a romantic novel from Mills & Boon®

Presents™ *Enchanted*™ *Temptation*®

Historical Romance™ *Medical Romance*™

MILLS & BOON®

Medical Romance™

COMING NEXT MONTH

A TRUSTWORTHY MAN by Josie Metcalfe

Sister Abigail Walker thoroughly enjoyed her work in the A&E department, even more so when Dr Ben Taylor arrived! But was Ben the trustworthy and gentle colleague she thought him to be...

BABIES ON HER MIND by Jessica Matthews

Midwife Emily Chandler had not intended to succumb to obstetrician Will Patton. Just because she found herself unexpectedly pregnant was no reason to marry him but Will had other ideas!

OUR NEW MUMMY by Jennifer Taylor
A Country Practice—the second of four books.

Dr David Ross was unprepared for his reaction to the arrival of Laura Mackenzie, consultant paediatrician. Was he betraying the memory of his wife or was it time to move on...

TIME ENOUGH by Carol Wood

Dr Ben Buchan's new locum, Dr Kate Ross, was making a determined effort to start her life again. But did that include becoming involved with the boss?

Available from 4th June 1999

Available at most branches of WH Smith, Tesco, Asda, Martins, Borders, Easons, Volume One/James Thin and most good paperback bookshops

Perfect Summer

The perfect way to relax this summer!

Four stories from best selling
Mills & Boon® authors

JoAnn Ross

Vicki Lewis Thompson

Janice Kaiser

Stephanie Bond

*Enjoy the fun, the drama
and the excitement!*

Published 21 May 1999

FREE!

2 Books
and a surprise gift!

We would like to take this opportunity to thank you for reading this Mills & Boon® book by offering you the chance to take TWO more specially selected titles from the Medical Romance™ series absolutely FREE! We're also making this offer to introduce you to the benefits of the Reader Service™—

- ★ FREE home delivery
- ★ FREE gifts and competitions
- ★ FREE monthly Newsletter
- ★ Books available before they're in the shops
- ★ Exclusive Reader Service discounts

Accepting these FREE books and gift places you under no obligation to buy; you may cancel at any time, even after receiving your free shipment. Simply complete your details below and return the entire page to the address below. *You don't even need a stamp!*

YES! Please send me 2 free Medical Romance books and a surprise gift. I understand that unless you hear from me, I will receive 4 superb new titles every month for just £2.40 each, postage and packing free. I am under no obligation to purchase any books and may cancel my subscription at any time. The free books and gift will be mine to keep in any case.

M9EB

Ms/Mrs/Miss/Mr ....Initials ....
BLOCK CAPITALS PLEASE

Surname...

Address...

....

....Postcode ....

Send this whole page to:
THE READER SERVICE, FREEPOST CN81, CROYDON, CR9 3WZ
(Eire readers please send coupon to: P.O. BOX 4546, DUBLIN 24.)

Offer not valid to current Reader Service subscribers to this series. We reserve the right to refuse an application and applicants must be aged 18 years or over. Only one application per household. Terms and prices subject to change without notice. Offer expires 30th November 1999. As a result of this application, you may receive further offers from Harlequin Mills & Boon and other carefully selected companies. If you would prefer not to share in this opportunity please write to The Data Manager at the address above.

Mills & Boon is a registered trademark owned by Harlequin Mills & Boon Limited.
Medical Romance is being used as a trademark.

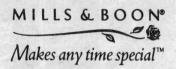

Trusting in James...

Returning to Yewdale was no hardship for
Dr Elizabeth Allen, for she loved the place and
its people. Working alongside her father at
their general practice was a joy, until his health
gave out and he retired. Change was
unwelcome to Elizabeth, so she wasn't
particularly welcoming to Dr James Sinclair
when he arrived – besides, James was a
Londoner; wouldn't he find Yewdale boring
and not give of his best to the patients?

Elizabeth soon realised how wrong she was,
but she found it very hard to admit her intense
feelings for this charismatic man, even though
he made his interest in her very clear!
But before they could resolve things, James's
ex-fiancée turned up...

Partnership and passion, love and
laughter at Yewdale Practice

UK £2.40

ISBN 0-263-81679-6

9 780263 816792 >

MILLS & BOON®

Makes any time special™